ET-BEINGS 10/8 ET-BEINGS & MAN-KIND SHARE the NEW EARTH...

Author:

John Q. Zarr ·>□ ·□

This book, like all my ET-BEINGS' books are dedicated to those who are insulted and/or seeking the True

WHAT IF?

and

Especially Margie, my soul/star mate whom we have been together in many times and many forms and rolls to each other...

What IF we can come around many more times together...to share more, and to learn more, and accept more from all the Universes'/Time Realms...

WHAT IF???

DISCLAIMER: I guess I need a "disclaimer here" This is listed as a book of fiction as all my ET-BEINGS books, DVDs, and/or classes; and since any of the main/or sub-characters can not be claimed as real or not there should be no confusions with real people. And since several major organizations of the world seem to have a very active denial process about characters and subjects I write about don't exist, and this appears as autobiographical and the conversations can not take place... then I feel I have a very strong disclaimer as to what is real and not real. However, any reference to any actually known person is strictly for reference only, and can be verified by multiple entries on the Internet, other books and news articles etc.

ET-BEINGS 10/8 ET-BEINGS & MAN-KIND SHARE the NEW EARTH... BEYOND???

That has to be a joke, right? No..."What's you talking about Willis?" Did they kill each other totally, and they all share the same hole in the ground?

TEACHER says I am being very humanistically emotionally sarcastic. I asked her do you know me to be any other way?

That stumped her for about 4 seconds

She said it was *A PREDOMINATE BEHAVIOR PATTERN OF MY BEING.*

That shut me up for about 7 seconds.

Okay changing the subject...remember when I told you the answer was "1" and very few), if anybody believed me...well, here's proof.

Divide 1 by ANY # as infinitively as you want and it is still 1 part of that number. No "0" will not work because "0" implies nuttin, zip, nada as in absolutely "not there." Asking about 2—infinity...well those can be divided down to "1" so thare youz has it...it's arzzz "1"..that's hillbilly speak as most people who make the news of seeing UFO's.

You can tell who they are, by no teeth and saying "I seen it over younder." The CIA are rumored to say "toothless hillbillies make the best witnesses for certifying UFO sightings." Now, you know why you hardly ever see intelligent reputable people being interviewed by the news as they are "NOT creditable certifying UFO witness."

BUT and a BIG BUTT! That was over approx. seven centuries ago and the time now is 2719, and the ET-BEINGS and present day man-kind both share the new earth together and both species though have "protective segregation laws" to ensure the earth is a safer, cleaner, friendlier, and much more highly technologically advanced world as in a homogenous operational productive society. "Bush finally got his thousand points of friendly lights."

WARNING: A LOT of this book you, the average person or pseudo-intellectual type are NOT going to like or even try to accept a lot of what is being written here....and you know how I feel about that. I must actually be honest with my "few readers (I am no fool I know I only have a few), that I sound like I am insulting you...to be honest I am only insulting you <u>if</u> it is true and please for all of us change that attitude to better yourself and the rest of us and the planet. I really do 'admire" the human being with all its faults, and that is what makes us ALL unique and that is what makes the Universe rotate.

Making mistakes and here is the rock/hard place point we have to learn from the mistakes so we can grow and advance, and not stay in the rut of no mental/emotional-physical, spiritual development.

My niece wanted to know why she always only met and got emotionally involved with "losers", and these jerk wads were losers from the very beginning. So I asked Laura (not her name), so you say your life is in a rut and you only meet and get involved with guys who have no respect for you and always hurt you?

Two questions…how much do you respect yourself and if you always travel in a ditch/rut what do you think you are only going to meet and get involved with? That was many moons ago…she is now been married for 12 years, has two great kids, a husband who not only really loves her and respects her but she is also an industrial engineer and supervises some very remarkable renewable product projects. I get a "hand written" Christmas card/letter from all of them (including Jerry—not his name), every year with an update on all the happenings.

How am I writing this in 2719…am I writing this in 2019…or?

Beats the heck out of me? All I, me, and myself know along with all those other dudes and dudettes in my gut is we all were making the final arrangements to communicate with the OTHERS in a secluded abandoned warehouse on earth as agreed.

The OTHERs can breath Oxygen earth's atmosphere and they agreed that I would be safer on earth for our meeting. They seemed very concerned that my safety of transport was as safe as possible.

Even though TEACHER and her kind were no-where to be seen or heard or telepathically communicated with. The trip cost me zero cents since one second I am in my rocker back home in Florida and the next second and I mean the next second I am standing in an abandoned warehouse somewhere in the middle of the desert somewhere on earth…I presume it is in the USA but I can not swear to that exact fact…there are several deserts on the earth.

Crap! the beer did not travel with me…I bet it is still sitting near the recliner and the damn TV is still on as they caught me by surprise as to the time of our meeting was scheduled at a different date and time…unless I messed up. I never could get GMT an UT time straight. If they just said EST or EDST I would have been a "little better prepared." I wonder if they validate parking for a refund on my electric bill?

Can you tell I am nervous...well I am hell ALL of us are nervous and my feet will not move even though my brain is saying RUN LIKE YOUR LIFE DEPENDS UPON IT!...my fear is that it does?

I am in the middle of this big open space and now I see what looks like a glow growing brighter into brilliance in a less than a second like a 25 watt light bulb just got juiced with a million volts. Absolutely cool and scary looking at the same time...oh shit I am not prepared for what just materialized.

GOD if you care anything about me do not let them be reading my mind right now.

WE PERCEIVE YOU.

I fall to my knees, with my hands covering my ears hoping to keep my brain from exploding. I yelled CHRIST ALMIGHTY ARE YOU TRYING TO KILL ME!!!

I am going to leave that there for a while...hopefully, I'll get back to it...if I don't oh well that's how the wall falls. Besides a spoonful of medicine makes the sugar go down easier, or something like that.

Let's semi-sort of begin where we moderately left off in ET-BEINGS 7/6 Truth Or the "Con-see-kwinches." Flat-out unequivocally true factual statement.

The New Earth, Man-kind and the ET-Beings are much better off after the asteroid burn the face of the earth than it was any other time in its history.

Dumb-ass man-kind learned how to make the laws and the ET-BEING help make the technology all thanks to the rich affluent families forking out the dough in interest bearing loans to the planet to rebuild and "fix" the planet.

In the first 500+ years the vegetation and the seeds of the surviving plants (way down deep in the earth), all sprung back with a ferocious appetite to grow, and prosper just like after a massive forest fire the plants come back quicker than ever. This made our blue marble planet green again and in areas where it was not green before.

This next part is where I could care less if you like it or not, but it is absolute major contributor to making man-kind and the planet a much better place. The mandatory rule of NO-MORE than two living children per couple. This present day fucking your brains out and the hell with the results was one of the first laws changed and was unceremoniously enacted and enforced by the

RFID chip alerting the body and the population control authorities to each and every pregnancy.

Abortions with the vacuum cleaner and veggie chopper were very out dated and actually against the law, and severely punished it anyone tried to do abortions the old in-humane way.

Technology was so advanced that within two hours of concievement (the body registers the hormonal changes alerting the monitoring systems of the RFID chip the zygote is aborted while the egg is very small, and the woman will totally be unaware of the abortion, except the small amount of blood when it is not her cycle. However, the birth control technology is 10,000 times a lot safer and more effective than it is in 2019.

Couples have to register to have or try to have a child. If a child or two children in the family are killed or dies in an "acceptable manner" then the couple are allowed to petition to have one or two more births. Just because they lose a child or two even if it is an acceptable manner (usually un-remarkable accidents), does NOT guarantee they will be granted permission to have additional births. And it is forced sterilization for both male and female if they try to have a child without permission.

And like it or not I am all for it...I just wish we had the laws and technology for this in 2019, instead of having to wait over 500 years and get our asses smacked by a big rock out of heavens to get our stupid idiotic attention and burn some brains in our hard heads.

That is just one of the many LOGICAL Laws that have been enacted and being enforced. We finally got smart and allowed the AI computers to write the laws and we voted on them as an unified planet.

What I liked is that if we didn't vote for the law as the AI computer wrote it we could "submit an alternative" and the AI computer would evaluate it to see if it met the requirements of what was written or had logical merit to be changed and re-voted on.

Oh, did I not say there was no fat cat CONgress "Poly-tick-shuns." Shame on me for omitting that little un-important tid-bit of information.

True they may have been rich and affluent before but they took a number just like everyone else did and NO-ONE did not have a RFID chip embedded near the heart organ.

I REALLY LOVE this law...computer hackers who tried to mess with anyone's RFID chip and got caught were not KILLED they were turned into living vegetables...totally aware of every day of their sorry life. They could not move, talk, however, they could hear and see everything around them as they lie in a bed unable to move their head staring at the same gray ceiling day after day, unable to feed themselves, and the IV feeds them and they can not pee or take a dump as mechanical wipers cleaned their ass from an inverted angle and the catheter so they could pee. The bed mattress moved air bladders to prevent bed sores. Hey we are not total tortures. So if you want to do the crime be prepared for the rest of your sorry life to do the TIME.

What I really like about the law, there is no plea bargaining and all the punishments are the same…"Life as a veggie who can see and hear but can't do anything else."

The RFID chip mandatory law from the moment of birth was the best law ever enacted. It was written by the AI computers and actually passed a majority of the vote. However, the law was going to be enacted and very aggressively enforced regardless of the planetary vote…the voting just made it a little easier to enact.

So how did the first series of RFID chips get installed when the rule was being enacted and enforced against all those that did not want to get chip.

Simple, I so LOVE this plan…all those that did not want the chip were given a three day pass to any nine exotic locations they wanted to go to before getting on the transport voluntarily to return to get the RFID chip. The AI robotic computers knew it took some people longer to "come to their senses than others" Thus the all expensed paid exotic vacation to any nine locations.

If you went on the trip and voluntarily returned to get your RFID chip no questions were asked and there was not repayment require.

After the transports returned (all nine) with whomever, returned all nine locations were totally obliterated by massive lasers satellites that had thermos detectors that could see a mosquito from space.

The offer was simple you can go to any of these 9 exotic locations and you can live there "till you DIE." The AI computers did NOT lie…they never said how long you can live.

A few "returnees" balked as the AI computers made the news open totally world-wide. However, 99.99% stopped "balking when they fell on the grown writing with sever heart pains and choking and the warning that says you can stop your pain by mentally agreeing to be a productive citizen." The few that could not/ would not agree soon died a painful death in a few hours, and were scooped up off the planet and "disposed of." The "families were allowed to say good-by and tried to get closure…However, as I said very few people actually died after returning and experiencing the tremendous chest pains. There never was a "balk" again.

The absolute best part is NO exotic place on earth was obliterated. The exotic trip, location and even the return voyage back was all in their heads. They never left the confines of the special "treatment facility." So no birds animals or fish were harmed in "correcting the attitude" of the non-conformist.

Yep, they were instantaneously turned to dust and left very little work for the robot janitors to clean, and polish and remodel the treatment area into a really nice retreat, for the living.

Warning is still in effect that pertains to a lot of this book.

What **WARS**! Are you respectfully crazy? IF you are truly crazy I mean no offenses...if not get real...that RFID chip if it was a "Planetary Law" this very day do you imagine how this real present day world would **CHANGE**!!!

One extra little note about wars or aggressive acts. What benefit is it IF you (the aggressor), attacks when EVERY developed nation with the enforcement of the planetary AI weapons (no need for human solders), from space will totally "vaporize" not only you but everyone one in your bloodline (coded in the RFID chip), from the face of the earth or whatever "Earth territorial possession where ever located). Vaporize as in no body, no pieces of scraps to be buried, no mess, no blood, bones...nil, zip nada as in never existed and as I said, this is true for your immediate bloodline as well. The third distant cousin in the bloodline may be spared...just depends upon the voting mood the AI Planetary Enforcement department feels at that moment.

ALSO very important...these RFID chips can not be blocked (with AL foil), like funky RFID chips now days. Centuries of research went into developing these babies, and they are pi # percentage fool-proof. That is a Huge infinity fool-proof percentage number.

But look at the present day jobs that would go into the toilet...especially lawyers...who have to actually "represent the person." But there are few very "punitive" laws. People who have an RFID chip that pleads not guilty and "legally" presents his case to the AI computer judge and a "HUMAN judge" Yep two judges hear the case and the ruling has to be unanimous by the AI judge and the human judge...if the human judge disagrees with the AI judge the person is placed on "Probation." The AI judge decides what time the probation period will be in effect.

HOWEVER, how do you plead "not guilty" when your RFID chip says oh yes, you are GPS located, videoed from satellite, drones, and the camera in the doorbell, and the street light documenting you were robbing the kid of his lemonade money when his back was turned.

You better hope the human judge decides probation for you to do community service, and the AI judge says 100 hours of making lemonade in the Sahara desert for free...you pay for the lemons and water. Hey, trust me the judgment could be a LOT harsher.

Oh yes, you pay the hourly rate for the judges, lawyer and the 100 hours estimated income for the kids lemonade...with a "spin the wheel multiplier"...you get to decide with the spin of the wheel to multiply 1— 50...there are also 00 in two places. So you could get a break with 00 or 1 in four places and the other numbers are in one segment. No one ever said the AI judges were not fair. So far No one has hit the 00 nor the 1s, yet...so "do you feel lucky."

WE TRANSMITTED ONE OCTAVE ABOVE TOTAL MINIMUM.

Well you damn near killed me!

WE WILL TRANSMIT AT THE MINIMUM DURING OUR COMMUNICATIONS.

Do you have a below minimum as my brain is being vibrated like a drop of cold water on a boiler plate every time you transmit.

WE WILL SEND TRANSMISSION TO ANOTHER CONSTELLATION BEFORE ROUTING TO YOU.

Thanks that sounds and feels acceptable. What is it...

WE EVALUATED YOUR ILLOGICAL ACTIONS FOR US TO MODIFY OUR EVALUATIONS.

Evidently you are understanding my thoughts as I think them?

YES, EVEN THOUGH VERY PRIMITIVE.

Well obvious present day human is not anywhere near advanced, and that is one reason why I presented my illogical evaluation request.

THE EVALUATION LOGIC OF INCREASING HUMAN DNA IS A PART OF OUR EVALUATION REQUIREMENT.

Is this in relationship to the visitor I call TEACHER and her kind?

WE ARE SEPARATE BUT PREDOMINATE EVALUATIONS ARE THE SAME.

NOTE: I have to do this in segments since communication with the OTHERs is a real pain in the head...I would say ass, but in this case they are not so interchangeable...in my humble opinion.

What is "Righteously Imbedded Freedoms Defender" (RFID) chip cons? Well, for one thing you can NOT do whatever in the hell you want, and not take responsibility for your actions. The chip documents your mental status as well and "verifies" if you are truly crazy and NOT responsible or not.

You can not call in sick and go to a movie, instead you have to take a very liberal personal time pass to go to the movie. Heck you only work 6 hours a day for three days straight or every other day depending upon you and your boss agreements. On top of that you have a full paid hour for lunch out of the 6 hour work day. Yes, some jobs are on 24/7 but there are plenty of people to fill the jobs and no-one is really over work or harassed or bullied at school or work. The RFID chip makes it very "painful" for those that think bullying or harassment is cool.

I guess a con would be there are no more violent gangs you can belong to...you are going have to find your need to "belong" in a more sociable acceptable ways.

I guess another con would be free medical coverage for life on any medical condition and there may be a waiting time of an hour before you can be seen by an AI medical evaluator/and a human coordinator. And trying to fake a heart-attack because you got caught "with your pants down" as they say is not going to get you off the hook for your behavior.

Another con and this is probably the most "human annoying" is that you are not in control and you do NOT make the rules and the rules apply to everyone, rich/semi-rich, less rich, and all the others everywhere, world-wide.

Plus the "richer" or more affluent you are the more social responsibility you have to the planetary communities...everywhere.

Yep, you guessed it... your taxes are higher as you are taxed at the flat 10% unless you are "filthy rich" over 100 million gold credits in you individual personal account... then you are taxed 12%...the super duper filthy rich ($1Billion+) gold credits in the individual personal account is taxed the max 15%, and there are no deductions on anyone's taxes. As the rate goes from 2% (lowest to 15%-highest), on every gold credit earned/spent. And only gold credits are taxed...silver credits for very unfortunates are not taxed at all. And don't think the silver can accumulate to massive amounts...NOPE the gold to silver ratio is fixed and every silver at the 50 level is converted to 1 gold, just to keep everything fair, and the entire planetary currency system tracks every person's transactions regardless where in the Universe you may be.

PROTECTIVE AGREED SEGREGATION: these areas are locations across the world where the ET-BEINGS reside and interact with special trained humans to understand and appreciate the unique life styles of the ET-BEINGS and their specific wants and needs.

These are MUTUALLY respected locations and as such with the AI protective enforcement systems and yes, the ET-BEINGS all have RFID chips. The special designed RFID chips were actually introduced by the True Beings like TEACHER and when presented to the humans the concepts took a little while to get used to and understood.

The biggest draw-back the humans had was the illusion of the right to privacy. Privacy is an illusion that we are all entitled to until our right over-runs someone else's right. No two rights do not make a right...nor a wrong.

Naturally, the ancient Constitution that the USA used and the other "constitutions" for the other nations all had to be ratified and amended as to what the word "RIGHTS and Entitlements actually mean?

RIGHTS was declared UNIVERSALLY that means other planets in the planetary court system stated that rights were those behaviors given freely to each (not person), but TO EACH without reprisal as long as no right over ruled another's' inalienable right(s).

Note: It took man-kind 1,235 years before they realized the irony of the word "in-ALIEN-able" really comprised of.

These **PROTECTIVE AGREED SEGREGATION** areas are NOT anything like we see in present day movies of segregation squallier camps worse than ghettos or the absolutely despicable Native American Reservation lands....NO sir these are nice, clean, safe, living/ working locations exactly like the everyday upper class humans have. The really affluent have it a little better and the really low "lower class" don't have it very much less either. There is no one or class of people that are not well cared for and taken care of since irresponsible reproduction, and strict population control, and all the destructive greedy behaviors of the old world are done away with entirely. All entities and the planet is a much better healthier place.

The advanced technologies that the ET-BEINGS brought back home to earth and man-kind have made all these advances and future advances possible.

The True beings as you remember from my conversations with TEACHER and her kind were already well advanced in time/space travel and so much more technology that provided man-kind astronomical leaps into space, time, and dimensional travel.

The real significance of the ET-BEINGS being the resultant of the future humans that left earth before the asteroid impacted earth and totally unaware of the events taking place on earth for hundreds of years while the small group were in cryo-suspension and being cared for by androids and cyborgs mixing and perfecting the new DNA chain.

In away the True Beings like TEACHER and her kind were the ancestors and the future forebears of present day man-kind. Or as TEACHER said...

SEPARATION AND LACK OF KNOWING OF OUR INDIVIDUAL EXISTENCE PROVIDED THE MOST LOGICAL PATHWAY FOR OUR INDIVIDUALIZED SPECIES TO JOIN IN TIME.

And now that joining is being shared by all on earth...and actually elsewhere as well.

OUR EVALUATIONS OF MAN-KIND AND PLANET ARE BEING EVALUATED TO PRODUCE MORE ACCURATE ANALYSIS.

Okay but please forgive me as you guys and TEACHER all seem to speak or communicate in the same double twisted logic to a typical human being.

IT IS YOUR INABILITY TO UNDERSTAND SIMPLE LOGIC THAT CONVOLUTES.

Well I can see we are going to be a trial and error method in our conversations.

AS WE UNDERSTAND YOUR INABILITY TO FORMULATE THE LOGIC THIS MEETING IS NOT PRODUCTIVE TO OUR EVALUATIONS.

Crap I am back in my chair...well maybe I am VERY thankful I am back in my chair, and not being kidnapped on some god knows what they travel in space ship to some far flung corner of the universe.

But geeze what a rude bastard that OTHERS dude was...he has to be a he because I hope to heaven the females are not that weird looking and actually creepy ugly. However, I am going to do some sketches of what the OTHER looked like, and hopefully I can learn more about them from hopefully another meeting. I did pick-up some images/information about their internal organs and composition when that............ whatever was blasting my brain. Universe willing, I will be around to share them with you. I did learn quickly why they look short, and then very tall almost at the same time...very unique leg structure, and those eyes (all three—one in back of head), are really weird. I don't think there are any "meat tearing teeth," thank God for that tid-bit. Of course it could be like the "Alien" in the movie with that sneaky quick in/out extra set of razor sharp shark teeth. They could be mechanical and hiding in that thing that looks like a fish tail goatee.

I need a drink!...join me if you want one, too?

Two ice cold beers later. I really like ice cold beer with ice crystals mixed in with the brew. However, having to live on a tight budget does not allow a lot of extras, so I buy the cheapest but decent tasting beer that is on sale. If I want exotic beer, I'll squirt a dash of lime or lemon juice into it and really exotic, I pinch some sea salt for a bitter taste....like those that cost a bunch more bucks. The snacks are usually home baked walnuts, almonds or pecans or peanuts in the table top convection oven, drizzled in raw honey, a smidge of butter and some seasoning including hot sauce, if I want "zinger nuts." But don't rub that shit in your eyes even if you think your hands are clean...wash them again just to be safe instead of (from experience), "tearfully sorry."

Okay, I've made some crude drawings of the OTHERS and I will try to "clean" these up before I share them, but I want to get back to that "ILLUSION" of privacy, freedom, free-will crap that man-kind lives under.

Yep, you guessed it...time to be insulted again...hell I was, too when I learned the pros and CONs of the system.

PRIVACY: let's look at the modern and the archaic definitions Definition of privacy: plural privacies...the quality or state of being apart from company or observation...seclusion... freedom from unauthorized intrusion one's right to privacy... archaic a place of seclusion...secrecy... a private matter as in secret.

Honestly ask yourself "when was the last time you REALLY had that"...you know the answer...NEVER! It is all smoke and mirrors and the mirrors are badly cracked, peeling and need replacing.

SO, does the RFID chip take away something you NEVER really had? No, it only makes the illusion less hidden.

I know you are going to say what about really personal matters like bathroom, showers, bed, and sexual relationships. You argue you have privacy there? DO YOU? Okay I am going to be generous and give you a benefit of a human doubt of a 5% correct answer. Even if your computer knows all about your bathroom breaks, and your TV can monitor your every movement in your house, and you think the camera is not watching you just because the little blue light is not on? Your security system in your home, and the fire systems, and the talking Internet with the sexy voice, and your refrigerator that tells you your milk stinks, and the car that starts to be warm inside when it's cold outside, while you are gulping your last bite of toast and coffee....and god who knows what all else we had before the great asteroid impact that "monitor" our every move and vital function like a 24/7 giant fitness watch that said your heart rate is increasing because you like looking at porn. The best part is you go an "brag" to all you social media contacts about your life...as IF everyone really cares or gives a shit, if yours stinks or not, or how many damn multiple orgasms you had with the illegal immigrant that cleans your pool and trims your "bushes."

Better get out the good mirror polish because this smoke and mirror trick of privacy is in really bad shape.

What's cheaper and more effective RFID chips with 100% enforcement in everyone from birth or trillions of dollars on cameras that have no enforcement and provide no protection. Sort of like a rubber with the tip cut off, and the rubber is just a penis sleeve at preventing disease or pregnancies. The "ribbed sleeve" may feel a little better but it ain't doing what it supposed to do...is it?

Hip Hip Hurray and Bang or Beat the drum slowly for the Conditioned Breeders. These undaunted unsung heroes and heroines of high octane breeders. They were the Conditioned Humans that were breeders on the star ships, but as things changed they were asked if they wanted to live on earth or other colonies or on the star ships. You may ask why would anyone choose the star ships? Well, what is the name "star ship" imagine all the billions of galaxies and wonders of the Universe they get to see, and sometimes when the atmospheres are safe enough for the Conditioned humans they get to experience even being on a new planet in a different universe...sign me up for that ship, I'll even pack my own tooth brush.

Those new discovered earth like planets if totally uninhabited by any "competitive life form" are presented to the planetary federation for consideration when we start to experience our sun is becoming a danger to our earth and/or solar system. Luckily that is still about another billion or so years before it starts getting really hot in the hood. By that time man-kind and the ET-BEINGS should have located several 1,000s or even tens of thousands of "goldilocks'" style earths in the universe and already have house and home established long before we MUST vacate earth because of the sun....asteroids are no problem anymore with all the modern technology. Besides 1,000s are being mined for water and minerals and other stuff as the major moons of the planets are actually resort vacation spots... as long as you are under the protective dome...we have not really terra- formed the moons to be like small earths, yet.

Okay you ask about FREE WILL. Did you read my other ET-BEINGS books? Free will is "tricky" based upon what our spirits agreed to before we ever walked the face of the planet and what influence's we were born under and what influence's our basic judgements based upon real or unreal perceptions, and a bunch more here and there stuff just to sweeten the indecisive world of free-will.

Since I covered free-will a lot in **ET-BEINGS 2 A TEXTBOOK, ET-BEINGS 3 the On-Going Final Chapters and** even here and there in **ET-Beings 4 and 5** I will not go into a lot of detail here. I do not like reinventing the wheel if you know what I mean.

We are bombarded with influence's 24/7 that negate anything close to free-will. Again another smoke and mirrors illusion polar trick but only this time it is us doing the fooling to ourselves based upon our perceptions of what we think is real unreal and what we want and do not want to believe or worst of all be able to blame. The devil made me do it...the hell he, she it did... you did it! Now do you know why, and can you accept the personal responsibility for what you did or why you didn't do what you should have done? Heck NO! Know why...because you DO NOT have Free Will...Never had it, and NEVER WILL HAVE IT!

So, does RFID chips preclude or interfere with FREE WILL? How?... since there is actually logically no such thing....it is a moot point since IT can not exist in the real world, as it is NOT tangible with all the variable influences.

Well I thought you took a much needed vacation since I have not heard from you for over two months...and only a few mental taps during that entire time.

WE AS ONE WERE ON AN ASSIGNMENT TO EVALUATE MAN-KIND'S FUTURE.

Are we talking about before the probable asteroid impact or after?

YES TO BOTH PROPOSALS.

Okay what did your evaluations determine?

LENGTHY REPORTS OF MINOR TO MAJOR PROBABILITIES WERE EVALUATED FOR FACTUAL LOGICAL CONCLUSIONS.

There you go again TEACH speaking in that damn double logic crappy way that you know confuses the hell out of me. Do you do that stuff on purpose...just to watch the convoluted brain waves train-wreck or what?

BRAIN WAVES AND RAIL TRANSPORT ARE NOT LOGICAL CORRELATORS.

Yeah, well they are to me and what they mean. Just make your statements short and to the point so a soft rock can understand them, and do NOT say anything about rocks not having intelligence to understand conversations because, I am using myself as the soft rock example.

MANY RECORDS WERE CHECKED AND VERIFIED AS FACTUAL FOR THE NEAR EARTH IMPACT ASTEROID AND THOSE THAT LEFT THE PLANET BEFORE AND WERE IN CRYO-STASIS DURING AND AFTER THE NEAR BY IMPACT FOR 439.22 EARTH YEARS AFTER.

The space ships that were build and were controlled and maintained by androids and cyborgs. Were these the same construction as on earth to monitor and maintain all the hospitals and other protective locations during and after the earth recovers from the nearby asteroid impact?

NO THE ROBOTIC UNITS ON THE SHIPS WERE 65% APPROXIMATIONS OF THE ROBOTIC UNITS ON EARTH AS THE ON-BOARD SHIP ROBOTIC UNITS TRAVELED MANY LOCATIONS ON RAILS AS THE EARTH UNITS WERE INDEPENDENT MOBILE AS THE ROBOTS ON BOARD THE SHIPS WERE PRIMARILY PROGRAMMED FOR THE CARE AND TREATMENT OF ALL LIFE FORMS ON BOARD WHERE THE EARTH UNITS WERE MORE LOGIC EVALUATION PROGRAMMED TO FUNCTION AS COLLECTIVE INDIVIDUAL UNITS EVALUATING THE EVENTS WITH LOGICAL ALTERATIVE COUNTER MEASURES OF PERFORMANCE.

Well, that actually makes sense and thanks for taking the time to explain in more direct easier to understand format.

COMMUNICATION THAT IS NOT UNDERSTOOD IS MOOT TO ALL.

Yes it is...so did you get into the events after the probable nearby impact or past those 425 years or so?

EVALUATIONS OF DATA RECORDS ARE BEING FORMULATED NOW AND REQUIRE ADDITION ANALYSIS.

So you have no idea how man-kind and you and your kind future progress past the earth's recovery time?

NO TO YOUR HYPOTHESIS WE HAVE DATA RECORDED IN YOUR FUTURE AS IN OUR PAST AS TO EVENTS OF OUR UNION-SHIP ON EARTH.

What? You and man-kind formed a relationship on earth?

NO I AS ONE DID NOT FORM THIS UNION AS THOSE AFTER ME ACTED AS ONE TO FORMULATED THE UNION OF OUR SPECIES.

So, I understand your physical self had expired? If that is true I am truly sorry for your demise.

WE AS ONE DO NOT DEMISE AS YOU STATED AS WE ARE PROGRESSIVELY CLONED.

So, a sequential number of your self was around for the creation and agreements for man-kind and True Beings to live and co-habit earth....together.

YES TO SEQUENTIAL UNIT AND NO TO YOUR STATEMENT OF FORMULATING THE AGREEMENT AS THIS UNIT WAS NOT INVOLVED IN THE PROCESS AS WE AGREED TO UNION-SHIPS ON EARTH AND OTHER PLANETARY LOCATIONS.

So you and man-kind shared the earth and other planets as well?

YES.

TEACH, I have a lot more questions for you but I am tired as these mental conversations seem to make me get more tired easier as I seem to get older and it gets more difficult for me to concentrate and really hear as in understand what I am perceiving from you and the others of your kind.

Thus ended the conversation with TEACHER. I was really glad to finally hear form her and find out the information that I did. To me it sounds like a "happy ending" so far but I still do not know how all this will correlate to me communicating with the OTHERs. However, that seems dead in the water as I have not heard anything back from the IMHO arrogant ass-hole creep. Even if it is 90% my fault for not being able to "understand" it...he could I feel try a little better to communicate with me as he should IMHO understand I am NOT as superior as he is, and therefore I am trying to do what I can to understand while working with a very severe handicapped disadvantage...jackass jerk!

Well, I think I will try to clean up some of these very rough sketches and put more "colorful" images of the OTHERS and their internal organs on paper.

Skeptics? Okay I hear the questions...what about those who are NOT implanted with a RFID chip? Honestly, in the year 2719 that there would be any way NOT to know if someone or thing did not have a RFID chip or other tracking capability. Do you think in 2719 that there are only a few ways of tracking? No offense...no I take that back...I intend to offend you if you really honestly think that.

There must be at a minimum 1,001 X 1,001 ways to track something or someone...everything from individual body smells (not BO), to weight upon the earth. I bet your life on it there are no ways to not be detected on earth and even most earth territories. Those less hospitable planets/locations are very harmful or deadly to living creatures if not inside a protected dome. Do you think that technology is NOT going to know if you belong in that protected dome or not?

The implanting and ENFORCEMENT of the RFID chip is a very serious deadly business as far as the earth, man-kind. ET-BEINGS and the planetary council is concerned and there are NO DO OVERS! Instant vaporization of the offender(s) and no plea bargaining except RFID hackers as I described earlier...they are life-long living veggies to suffer everyday of their natural life. Hackers have no living human association, just cold basic care robots who are programmed to make sure you stay alive and suffer as much as possible without bed sores.

Do I wish we had those systems/laws now in 2019..your damn straight I do!!! And you would too, if you looked at it logically, non-polluting/emotional crap. However, we can't yet, because our technology is not purified yet enough to make or enforce those laws and systems...just wishful thinking on me, myself, and I part.

So, looking at and being in the present where are we and where do we stand or our position of existence as TEACHER would say.

I am sure if you are a reader of the ET-BEINGS books or attended any of my classes that I do not write about all that TEACHER and her kind and yes even the OTHERS have shared with me...especially when it comes to technology that can and WILL actually take man-kind far into the future from this present day position.

Dumbass idiotic present day man-kind can not play nice in our terra-firma sand box and now we want to do exactly what I said in **ET-BEINGS A Report On Extraterrestrial Communications** and take our greed/hostilities into space. Thankfully right now it is fairly well situated just near earth and not to the outer reaches, yet...but give our stupidity time it will be there as I have pointed out a many of times in different ways and writings.

As I said, and will resay many times and in many, many different ways it is time present day man-kind and the planet paid a little more attention to reality as it is generally perceived and a lot less to social media who gives a shit about garbage...........garbage in GARBAGE out! Remember that on your way to the burial dump.

Defending our space resources is not really rocket science...again smoke and mirrors...or mirrors principles to be exact. No, I am not talking about big hunks of glass in space...we have better, much, much lighter and more effective technology than that right in my thermal blanket.

That strong as steel MYLAR is fantastic stuff when applied "logically" to our satellites. And with the ground based lasers we have today on harden rails and bunkers are fantastic. PLUS an added bonus when not being used to defend our satellites and others resources in space can be used to generate clean renewal able power actually for existing boiler generators we have on the planet right now.

HOW? You ask...well I'll be damn if I tell you...you want to know how to save/protect over 90% of our space resources and to generate clean power here on earth efficiently and cheap...your crazy as dodo bird if you think I am going to write it out here....you want to know then it you will need to sign some iron-clad non-refutable project development contracts.

I gave away billions of dollars worth of technology in **ET-BEINGS 5 When You See PREMA You See PRETA and ET-BEINGS 7/6 Truth or the Consequences.** It is all there all you have to do is develop and produce the damn stuff. The information on renewable energy, transportation and medical and saving the brains of your children it is all there and in other ET-BEINGS books as well.....Free to you and the world, but not the Space Force Protective and Counter Insurgent technologies.

Listen there is NOT ONE thing you can DIS-PROVE in my ET-BEINGS books and/or classes.....everything I have written is being formulated in one way or another. Realize it or not you are being given a map to man-kind's future. It is up to you to seek the WHAT Ifs any of this is true or not.........

Okay let's look at some other stuff that is pertinent to **ET-BEINGS and Man-Kind Sharing the New Earth.**

What about everyday lives of "everyday folks" who are not the True Beings (which I'll try to get into later).

Well, the everyday life is not very much like life was in 2019. Life in 2719 has real true value which is valued and appreciated by all; and it has very little to do with the RFID chip. That thing is basically not even considered a part of life since it has been implanted a few seconds after birth...and that includes the very, very rare "still births." That way every-body has a permeant chip ID # assigned to it. However, IF a "dead body chip" appears in the system then the AI RFID chip enforcement department goes into action, and does not stop till they find the error or why there is a dead body chip activated...especially since ALL dead bodies are supposedly cremated and ashes are launched into space as a " ceremonial act of getting man-kind closer to the Great Creator."

There is no funeral cost for the family as this is a community service the affluent is paying through their gold chip tax collection program...just like the gold chip taxes pay all medical and emergency care costs, too.

Everyday living is in very well developed apartments with interactive 6 D Virtual Reality and Alternative Reality screens and hollow laser imagery scenery programs. One day you can have mountains and snow and the next digging for gold in the dessert all from the comfort of your automatic adjusting form fitting recliner chair that molds to whomever is sitting in the chair in less than a minute.

Healthy real food of real plants and healthy synthetic meat of steaks, chickens and pork are all replicated in a special replicating grilling baking cooking oven in biodegradable plates and eating utensils that go into the master disposable slot that is burned to an ash by plasma heat and that ash is mixed with a natural resin to make a new plate spoon, glass casserole dish or what have you. Since the veggies are all natural and the meats are all synthetics, the food is very good healthy and does not taste like tofu turkey burger crap. The beverages are all natural (even carbonated), and no phosphoric acid crap or aspartame garbage and its Alzheimer causing qualities. Just like our toothpaste causes brain lesions today, there is none of that cancer or cell damaging stuff anywhere.

These changes all contribute to the average life span of a normal 2719 human being to be around 300 years...there are a few old dudes who are pushing 400.

Job stress is virtually nill as your body is monitored by the RFID chip and if your position in life is too stressful for you at that time you are authorized to take a break from the task till the blood pressure and other stress factors reduce. If they do not reduce within an hour the RFID chip notifies the management that you are being relived of your duties and will be driven home or to a medical evaluation facility for a more through analysis. Again, all this is at no cost to the everyday status class, and is paid for by the taxes of the gold credits.

Also most everyday class labor jobs are as I said are 6 hours a day with a full 1 hour lunch and two 30 minute breaks for 3 days of work in a the still seven day work week.

It was suggested by a "time management think tank" to convert the work week to 9 days based upon the 3 day or every other day work schedule. That 9 day work week calendar almost got past but, it conflicted with other laws and old sciences, too much. However, they are at it again, with a new marketing program, and it looks like it will get past since it involves the planetary possession's as well, instead of just earth time tables.

Flying robotic controlled transports and really super fast maglevs of over 1,000 miles an hour that are in vacuum tubes so there is no air resistances and having to deal with all those negative super high speed design concerns.

Special seats that face opposite of the direction of travel and they swell ont the padding as the train rapidly decelerates to a very comfortable loving embrace. Each seat measures the passengers specific body safety needs and conforms just like the body molding recliner does in your living room.

Bathrooms on the high speed maglevs are very unique... you get up out of your seat traveling 1,000+ mph and stand on the personnel conveyor that supports you safety to/from the bathroom. If you are in the toilet when stopping for a station (normally the maglevs are direct to/from destinations), but there are a few lesser used stop points, and your in the toilet (sitting/standing), a large three legged support comes up and around you to help reduce the stopping effect. It is not as comfortable as the seat but it saves your ass from being slammed into the toilet wall...even though you were told three times to return to the safety conveyor/seat before stopping.

The acceleration in your seat is like a rush/thrill but realistically very little physical effect because of all the safety technology in the seats. The bathroom thrill could scare the piss out of you...so, if your having problems going just wait till the rapid acceleration...that should clear your personal plumbing problems.

Buildings are virtually underground as much as they are above ground. Sure mother nature still has her volcanoes and earthquakes etc., but riding one of these shakers out is not a lot of damages due to really high tech earthquake technology, and the predictive early warning systems for seismic location/activity.

Glass is not your standard breakable stuff...it bends and twist and is actually stronger that present day steel, and most places of real significance have magnetic force fields surrounding the location making each area a small force field protected environment. Highly technical locations not only have the force field around the location but the highly trained tech works have personal protective force fields around them as well. If for example a really super bad disaster hits and the building actually comes apart and pieces begin to fall...well individuals will be safe from deflecting the falling debris with the individualized force field. However, that is virtually a nil ever happening scenario.

Fashion is simple most men and women wear the "sheik" garment. The human body needs natural air flow around all parts and men and women both learned that pants and other restrictive garments prevented natural air flow for the body (especially the gentiles), and that is why the open sheik garment is basically world-wide style of dress but that does not prevent it from being decorated and full of colors and designs. When women realized it eliminated the need for those damn pantyhose, girdles and body shapers etc. the style was rapidly picked up. Most men love going "commando" any way.

There are independent fashion rebels who wear pants and very short micro skirts with underwear leggings. Oh ladies high heels are virtually non-existent even by the fashion rebels and all the problems they caused. However for some damn reason girls wear them in the porn movies as the heels automatically rise and fall in height at a push of a button.

We still have porn in 2719...well yeas and no....Virtually reality allows you to program whatever you want to watch in the protection of your own home and even "hard core pedophile stuff, SM and other stuff including snuff porn is monitored by the RFID chip, and is not interfered with in any way at all...as long as it is in Virtual Reality. In VR you are free to be whomever and whatever you or a group choose to be. You can actually be 250 year highly sexed starved swingers who latterly have sex swinging from the trees with whomever you choose. You want to have sex with the president well put on your VR units and get in your body molding recliner and......well use your imagination. Ooops there are no ploy-tick-shuns in 2719....YEAH! YAHOOOOO!!!!!

Okay let's digest the years because, I know some of your really smart astute seekers of the What If are adding and subtracting the dates I keep referring to. However, there are dates I have not referred to as of yet that TEACHER has shared with me as to probable future events.

So after the probable near asteroid impact with earth near the end of the 21st century and then the earth self-rehabbing itself while the androids and cyborgs looked after and cared for those on the space ships outside earth's orbit a safe distance away from earth and any possible debris damages etc. the earth took almost as TEACHER said 500 hundred years to rehab itself back to a safe beautiful green planet with the man-made mutating virus fully destroyed not only by the cyborgs but also by the plasmatic fire produce by the glancing near miss asteroid. This was all pre-planned before the affluent left earth with the specific seeds in the space ships and placed into cryo-suspension.

This is approx. 2547 (not like "Zager/Evans song "In the Year 2525"). The song is really cool...you should listen to it on U-Tube. However, the space ships did not return until around 2570—2579. This started man-kinds rebirthing on New Earth. Those adults and children in cryo-suspended stasis were awaken first and these are the generations that made the laws of the RFID chips along with considerable information from the AI computers on how to make the New earth better and not do the same mistakes that were done in the past. These programs took almost 200 more years thus bringing us to 2719.

I have already written a lot about 2719 dates and those in the near future past 2719 but, TEACHER and her kind have not arrived as of yet. ET-BEINGS and man-kind do not start sharing the New Earth until around 3206. However, the AI systems androids and cyborgs were very aware of the ET-BEINGS presence around 2980 as they (ET-BEINGS), were in the "elder developmental phase."

How you ask did they know on New Earth? The electronic entities all communicated with each other after the New Earth was repopulated and this was after the small group of humans who left went to find another livable planet.

Yes, this small group of scientist and "humanitarians" were REBELS as they did not band with the affluent or go along with killing the populace with the mutating diseases.

By being rebels and independents their fate was virtually sealed as their destiny would be modified humans into the ET-BEINGS, or True Beings like TEACHER and of many of her similar kind.

So. TEACHER did you make the pyramids?

YOUR QUESTION IS FACTUALLY INCORRECT.

You can read my thoughts, you know exactly what I am talking about...did you make the pyramids in Egypt?

NO WE AS ONE IN OUR FAMILY.

Okay double speaking and hidden messages not said, do you know who made the pyramids?

YES.

Well? I am wanting and waiting for an answer.

WE AS ONE IN FAMILY DID NOT AS OTHERS IN THE HIVE PROVIDE TECHNICAL ASSISTANCE WITH LEVERAGES.

Okay, let my little human brain get a handle on what you just said. First I understand that you and your immediate family...those that have similar hand markings as you did not assist in building the pyramids but others in the hive did.

YES TO YOUR STATEMENT OF MY FAMILY ID AND NO TO YOU UNDERSTANDING OF THE HIVE STATEMENT.

So, it was not others in your hive that built the pyramids?

NO TO YOUR UNDERSTANDING OF BUILDERS.

TEACH, I am confused...if your hive did not build the pyramids as you said earlier then how could the hive build them and not build them?

YOUR UNDERSTANDINGS ARE CONVOLUTED.

Well damn it un-convolute them!

SEGMENTS OF YOUR UNDERSTANDINGS AND STATEMENTS ARE PREDOMINANTLY NON-FACTUAL.

Okay....TEACHER...let's take the convolutes apart one little piece at a time and get them factual. Did your hive build the pyramids?

NO.

Even though earlier you said it was your hive...then who built the pyramids?

THOSE OF THE LAND.

Would that be the slaves?

PREDOMINATELY YES.

So, humans built the pyramids but you said the hive built them?

YES TO HUMANS, NO TO HIVE BUILDING AS THE HIVE COMMUNICATED THE USE OF MOVEABLE LEVERAGES.

Okay if I dissect what you said piece by piece then I understand that the pyramids were basically built by humans that were what we called slaves in Egypt and your hive communicated I am presuming telepathically with the um...designers or mathematicians that were responsible for getting the pyramids built. Am I right so far?

YES.

Good that is a beginning. What is moveable leverages that was communicated to the designers?

THE CONSTRUCTION DIRECTORS WERE COMMUNICATED IMAGES AS TO MOVEABLE LEVERS THAT TRANSLATE IN AN AREA OF 270 EARTH DEGREE MEASUREMENTS FROM ONE LOCATION TO THE OTHER POINT OF INTERCEPT.

I think I understand what you said...you are aware of the very long narrow cranes we use to build buildings?

YES.

Is moveable leverages like a long boom cranes of present day technology?

PREDOMINATELY YES.

TEACH, how was the ancient pharos of Egypt able to use 21st century technology without 21st century construction material like steel and concrete and other modern day building stuff like carbon fibers? It just does not add up mentally.

NATURAL FIBERS ARE VERY STRONG WHEN APPLIED PROPERLY.

But those stones weighted tons...I mean 40—70 tons or more?

YES.

For god's sake don't just say yes...How were they moved so far?

PRINCIPLES OF REDUCED FRICTION WITH NATURAL RESOURCES AND MOVEABLE LEVERAGES.

Okay the pyramids are there that is a fact and that means 1,000s of years ago they were actually built. But the how is what is so puzzling to present day man-kind....can we call it a "time-out" for a while because I am getting really tired and I do not want to miss any small segment of what you have to share.

Thus ended that portion of the session with TEACHER and my mental fog of understanding about the pyramids was getting thicker....and I mean thicker because a few moments after we stop our conversation I had a thought about all the other pyramids that were built all over the earth. Holy crap now I am really confused...I need a drink...maybe two.

Dear reader put yourself in my shoes/recliner you and I are sitting here chillin and enjoying a drink or two (your choice), and we have a conversation about pyramids and math.

We seem to already established that the Mayans, Incas and those in that area had a different circle/pi # than what the Greeks, Romans and all those dudes on that side had. True as it may be it is only the ratio of 1:1.0013 difference. There we go again "13" even if it is 13/10,000s one of my three favorite #s (9 & 27 are my others), there again. I have made a lot of math games using 9--13 and/27 independently or together. I have been told I should market and sell them. Maybe I will after I close out the ET-BEINGS series.

Hint 13 and 27 have a LOT to do with Artificial Intelligence, VR and AR and oh that buzzard Mono-Polarity, too. It will get you into "Tachyon Hyper-Drive."

So how do you move all those tons of rocks and how did a little skinny guy who was 5ft 8inches tall move stones in Coral Gables Florida all by himself when he build Corral Castel as a tribute to the woman who broke his heart. What did Edward Leeskalnin mean when he said, "He figured out the secrets of the pyramids."

However, I must be honest with you...there are some very good U-Tube videos on "ole ED." I must confess I was very personally impressed with my times I have been to Corral Castle and my aura energy field measured 21 ft. from center...even though that is not technically a record...the people who manage Corral Castle were very impressed as most peoples' aura's energy fields are less than 3 feet.

Just a note...Ed took almost 28 years (as in 27.9) years to build Corral Castle. There's 27&9 again in a "woo/woo place, again. Also the beginning of new math of 9 is just the beginning. Trust me on this...it will require the Indigo Children to think in cubic not squares. Remember, that real Virtual Reality and Alternative Reality is in 6 dimensions. See other ET-BEINGS books.

I think I'll bug TEACHER about Crop Circles, too...I want to know more facts about them, also as to who what and why about the legit ones, and not all the beautiful "man-made phonies."

Why 3206 and not sooner...easy to answer hard as hell to explain.

Simple answer is that man-kind and ET-Being kind were NOT ready to share the new earth in total peace and harmony. Remember humans from earth are still human and all their illogical emotional garbage is still there as well. While the logic only ET-BEING is still totally logical and non emotional in a very constant battle to be logically emotionally. The conflict of the ET-BEING to be emotional in a logical state is a hell of a desire. Man-kind is almost just as messed up as he always is even in the year 3206 and beyond.

I hear you asking what is "Emotional Logic?" that is tricky to answer, and I am not even sure TEACHER can express it where it is understood but, we as one as she says will try to do what we can to clear up the mud and pitch-blend.

TEACHER, I hear you a lot of times saying you want to be an advanced human with what seems like a total contradiction of emotional logic. How is that possible and please for all of us soft rocks and you know what I mean please be specific detailed and as simple in your explanations as you can be...Okay?

ADVANCED HUMAN STATE IS BEYOND WHAT HUMAN PERCEIVEMENT AND REACTANCE LEVEL IS PRESENTLY.

Are you saying 2019 or 2719 or 3206 level?

3206 LEVEL.

Okay we are talking about something which is many centuries from where I am now correct?

YES IN YOUR PRESENT PHYSICAL STATE OF EXISTENCE.

Don't confuse me unless it is absolutely necessary, and then why would it be necessary?

CONFUSION DOES NOT PROMOTE UNDERSTANDING.

Yep...so let's keep it simple okay...remember you are communicating with soft rocks mentally.

WE AS ONE UNDERSTAND YOUR SOFT ROCK COMPARISON EVEN THOUGH IT IS NOT LOGICAL AS THAT IS A BASIC OF EMOTIONAL LOGIC.

Whoa what you just said makes sense and is beginning to clarify some of the basic confusions. If I understand correctly that information perceived even if it is not logical can be analyzed and rationalized as to a "logical understanding?"

YES TO PREDOMINATE UNDERSTANDING OF YOUR STATEMENT.

Good very good now we are getting somewhere...

WE ARE NOT MOVING.

TEACH it is a figure of speech as in understanding more as more information is provided.

WE AS ONE WILL DOCUMENT THAT STATEMENT AS TO UNDERSTANDING WHAT YOU CALL SLANG FOR UNDERSTANDING.

Umm, TEACH isn't that more like being a robot per se' than being human with all its complexities?

NO.

How there is no logical way to answer that question any other way?

NO TO YOUR STATEMENT OF ROBOTIC AS IN ONE OF OUR PRIMARY MISSION GOAL IS THE INTEGRATION OF ARTIFICIAL INTELLIGENCE AS YOU CALL IT INTO LOGICAL ASSESSMENT ANALYSIS.

TEACH, if it is not AI then what is it in your terms?

CORRELATION OF DATA AS TO A LOGICAL PROBABLE RESULTS.

Okay what you just said is actually what AI is as in answers simplified down to 0s and 1s., as in all machine languages the basic is all 0s and 1s. is it not true that all program languages regardless of the complexities are all based upon the very basic machine language of 0s and 1s?

YES TO YOUR PRESENT DAY PROGRAMMING FUNCTIONS AND NO TO THE ADVANCED THAT REQUIRES ADVANCED SUBATOMIC LEVEL COMPUTING.

You're talking about the fuzzy world of quantum?

UNAWARE OF THE FUZZY AS IN QUANTUM COMPUTATIONS AS TO PROBABLE
LOGIC IN RATIO TO ILLOGICAL ANALYSIS.

It's what the present day experts call quantum physics as "fuzzy logic" but to be honest I think the experts don't understand it enough to be definitive about how it works therefore, they call it fuzzy, because it is mentally fuzzy to their understandings and interpretations. So how is the fuzzy logic I just explained to you or the quantum any different from what we term Artificial Intelligence?

THE EVALUATION OF THE LOGIC AND ILLOGICAL TO PRODUCE A PROBABLE
RATIO ANALYSIS IS NOT FUZZY TO US AS ONE.

Touché' so you are saying because you are smarter than present day man-kind mentality or technology status it is not "fuzzy" to you or your kind.

YES.

Ouch.

WE DO NOT REGISTER ANY OF YOUR STATED PAIN.

No, no real pain just a punch in the emotional gut.

WE DID NOT REGISTER AN IMPACT WITH YOUR BODY.

No teach, it is slang for.....um.... oh forget it I don't know how to explain being mentally knocked down in the dirt, and don't say anything about not perceiving...it is something that will take a lot of explaining, and it is not worth all the time or effort to get you and your kind to understand what I am trying to say...you just have to be human to understand it and that is it in a nut shell.

COMPLEXITIES THAT ARE CONVOLUTED.

Exactly!...so, from what I understand I think, is that to you and your kind the intelligence is not artificial as in that all intelligence regardless if organic or mechanical is intelligent, and there is no differentiation as to real or artificial but only as to the level the intelligence functions.

YES.

Damn, I actually understand that...I am going to speculate here and project a thought that with that hypothesis of understanding that it eventually makes it easier for man-kind to accept robots in society.

YES A VERY NEEDED RELATIONSHIP FOR FUTURE MAN-KIND'S SURVIVAL.

Is that where the acceptance of androids and cyborgs began?

YES.

But not ET-BEINGS or OTHERS?

YES.

I guess one small step forward is better than no steps or backwards.

WHO IS TAKING THE STEPS AND WHERE DO THE STEPS LEAD AND THERE ARE MANY COMPLEXITIES TO YOUR STATEMENT.

I'll explain later...how about we close for now as I am getting tired and TEACHER do not let me forget I want to talk with some more about all this and more, and also I got a lot of questions on legit crop circles as we call them.

Thus ended the conversation with TEACHER and I was actually feeling some what relieved about this last conversation as I could actually begin to see the light at the end of the tunnel...then my warped me, myself and I and all those others joked about hope to GOD it is not that "here today and gone the next second" light at the end of the tunnel, if you get my drift...Oh well, I better get a cold one before I "shuffle-off" to...............oh, crap...... where??? I think I'll just take a nap.

Days later....what do you mean "river mucous and natural plants?"

AN ABUNDANT AMOUNT OF NATURAL GREEN REEDS AND RIVER MUCOUS PREDOMINATELY REDUCED THE FRICTION OF STONE MOVEMENT.

Um are you saying that a lot of small green natural water reeds and the slime from the bottom of the river made moving those super heavy stones easier?

YES.

Why green?

WEIGHT TO MEASUREABLE DISTANCE WAS DISPLACED BY MANY SUPPORTIVE POINTS AS THE MUCOUS PREDOMINATELY PROVIDED A VISCOSITY MIXED WITH HONEY FIXED A THICK WATER BARRIER TO THE STONE AND SUPPORTING GREEN ROLLING REED.

I'll be damn honey and water together made a very thick slick barrier between the stone blocks and the small green reeds lifted the stone just enough to allow the thicken mucous to provide a very slippery slope for the stone to move. Do I have that part correct?

YES.

So what is the moveable leverages?

FROM THE CENTER THE STONES CAN BE LIFTED PREDOMINATELY MORE ACCURATELY WITH LESS ENERGY REQUIRED.

TEACHER can you mentally show me what this looked like?   HOLY COW! That is remarkable and I see how the height increased without having to get taller support poles...WOW! It is actually very simple and now I understand how these huge pyramids could be built in what seemed to be an impossible short time span.

Gosh TEACHER thanks for that information.......Note to reader want to see drawings that explained how Egypt built the pyramids so fast? I have included some basic drawings for our education.

Reader do NOT delude yourself pulleys were easily made by sawing the tree stump into thirds. By taking the smaller dia. of the tree stump and trimming it to a circle was easy for these master craftsmen. Taking the smaller dia. and place two larger dia. circles on each end makes a perfect large pulley wheel. The large the diameter of the pulley and the more pulleys in a block and tackle system the less energy to lift and move what seems like impossible weights but it is not. Remember the old Atlas God saying..."Give me a place to stand, and I will move the EARTH."

Well with math, science and common logic those pyramids were built as proof today we see them. Hope you enjoy the drawings and realize you are a few of the world's populace who know how simple it was to be done....and you don't need no PhD to understand it either. Thanks Teach, we all really appreciate you and your kind sharing this information.

The following few pages explain who and how easy it was for a bunch of people working together to build these pyramids, and I already know that a lot of "experts" are going to find every little nit picking fault with my information that TEACHER shared with us. Do I care...not any more than a fart in a F- 5 dust devil. I would be very honored if the experts took that much effort and time to disprove me...How can we lose? Just for spite...I double dog dare you to prove me wrong!

Or as one of my Arkansas cronies says, "I did not have sex with that woman...you weren't there." So I ask you where does the truth separate from fiction....if at all...and there it is and what is the definition of IS?

The pyramid foot print is laid out first in stone except for middle sections entrances/exits for the lifting TRI-POD hoist tackle system. That is not laid out for you to see, nor is it exactly to scale but darn close. If you "study the next few drawings logically you will see who and how the Egyptian pyramids were built.

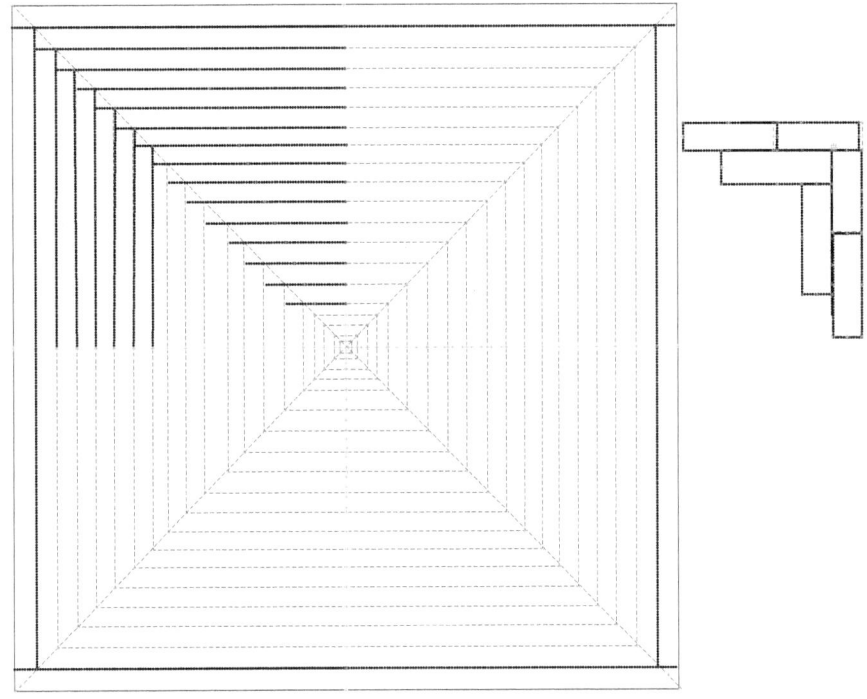

Notice the floor blocks meet at the corners in a square design and the blocks are staggered to meet in the middle just like we lay most bricks now days. This little bit of information is very important to the overall design and construction to the pyramids. Plus don't forget about what TEACHER already said about river mucous/honey and natural green reeds etc. to reduce or virtually nullify friction. By having the massive stone block lifted only a fraction of an inch on the slippery thick mucous/honey barrier mad it a lot more easier than you would think to move 40—80 TONs or more.

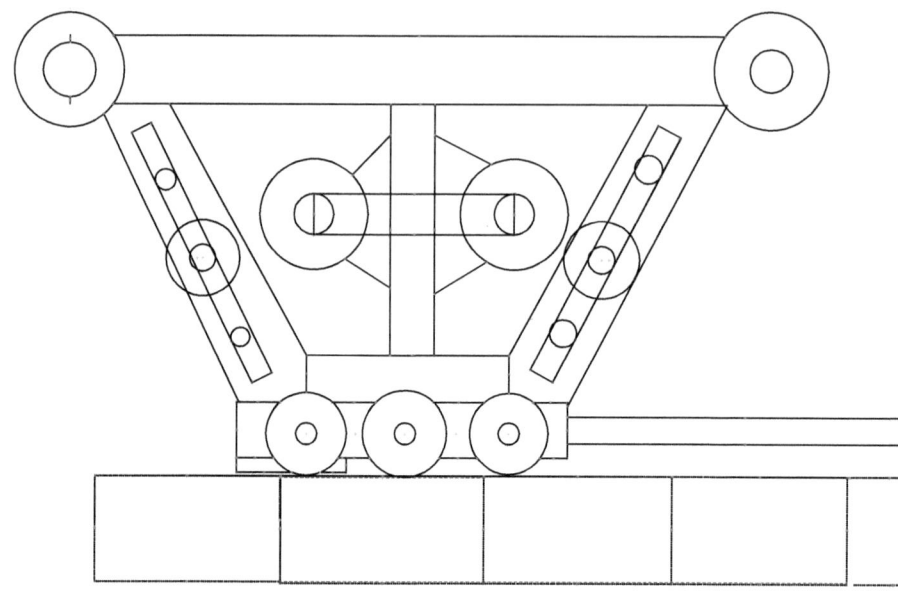

ET-BEINGS 10/ 8 Moveable Leverage Block Tackle unit

I am not going to explain very much about this very neat design as I think it is my design based upon what I read on the pyramids. I will say two things. 1st. the long push/pull tow bar moves the unit with human power, and 2nd as the wheels/axel rotates they act as pulleys as well. The Cyprus tree unit is very unique as it can easily lift over a 100 tons or more. A lot depends upon the natural hair and plant fiber rope holding strength. Hint take note of the sliding pulleys…..and if you were the design "foreman" where would you have the lifting rope/beam?

How many "mechanical advantages" do you count if you read how the "lifting mechanism" are utilizing many lifting combinations including the unique lifting mechanical advantages utilizing the wheel axels.

So do you want to go and "build your own pyramid" now you know how easy it is? Should give the universities something to really play with. Wonder if I can get some baubles/stiffens…"please sirz, I wuld like sum more?"

TEACHER, this has been bugging me and 1,000s maybe 100,000s of people want to know who makes the crop circles and what do they mean?

WE AS ONE DID NOT CONSTRUCT YOUR CROP CIRCLES AS YOU CALL THEM AS WE ARE VERY AWARE OF THESE GRAPHIC CONSTRUCTIONS.

TEACH, if you and your kind did not and do not construct these graphic constructions, do you know who does make these?

PREDOMINANTLY YES.

Well who or what is it?

The New Earth and planetary counsel with and without the co-habitation of the ET-BEINGS with man-kind is an on-going developmental process as man-kind is still human, and does not trust anyone or anything that is not exactly like the majority of the "controlling party or image." Hell, the human is still trying to understand and appreciate the android/cyborgs, even though they SAVED the human's ass so many times, and made the NEW EARTH so much BETTER!

Even in 3206 it is still an on-going understanding and appreciation process of both "SUB-species," even though they both are humans in one form or another, through all these centuries. What will the years or even centuries beyond 3206 will be as man-kind and the ET-BEINGS share the new earth...new earth as in probable asteroid impact.

Ask what does the seeds have to do with the seeds in the world seed bank before the impact? Well, that means I did not fully explain the seeds of living creatures. The seed count that I gave you before did not take into account the millions of plant species that were in cold storage at the world seed vault. There was an entire section devoted to each ship with multiple generations of the same seed in case there were some serious malfunctions of a space ship. Having all the seeds from the seed vault did not make logical sense to have located on just one ship. What would happen if something went haywire or the ship got contaminated or was actually destroyed...all of mankind's seeds and future plant growth would be lost. Luckily for all the space ships that the affluent built with the tremendous technical skills of the androids and cyborgs no space ships were loss. As stated there were less than 2% total loss of all humans and human seeds and plant seeds total loss on all the ships. That is a remarkable percentage of success as opposed to the tremendous amount of losses experienced on earth with the diseases and the after effects of the probable nearby asteroid impact plasmid fire and damage done to the atmosphere and its recovery time.

Strangely the horseshoe crab survived this devastation as well as it did the time the dinosaurs ate the dust with the results from the last huge meteorite or asteroid or even small planet impact millions of years ago.

GRAPHIC DESIGNS ARE OF OTHERS.

You mean that jackass that I dealt with before, his kind do the crop circles.

THE DONKEY OFF-SPRING CAN NOT MAKE THE GRAPHIC DESIGNS AS IT IS NOT FEASIBLE.

Okay...okay do you mean the OTHERS that rattle my brain when he communicated with me?

PREDOMINATE NO AS FAR AS OUR DATA PROVIDES.

Whoa, then what others?

SINCE YOUR RF TRANSMISSIONS YOUR PLANET IS VISITED BY MANY RESEARCHERS.

Oh great...we really are Grand Central Station to the universe.

NO. PREDOMINATE COSMOS DOES NOT VISIT EARTH AS NO PRIORITY TO THEIR NEEDS.

TEACH, you just said many visitors visit earth did you not?

YES.

Well what do you mean predominate of the cosmos then do not visit earth?

MANY REALMS OF EXISTENCE ARE NOT INTERESTED.

Okay so you are saying that some but not most universe visitors are not interested in earth to visit or research?

YES.

I guess that is a good thing....isn't it? To me it is if most are like that OTHERS dude I tried to communicate with.

IN YOUR TIME SPAN OF THE UNIVERSE OF 14.734 BILLION YEARS THE SOLAR SYSTEM SUN OF EARTH IS ONLY A 1/3 OF THAT EXISTENCE PROVIDING MANY SPECIES OF ADVANCED DEVELOPMENT FAR SUPERIOR TO OTHERS WHO VISIT YOU FOR RESEARCH EVALUATION PURPOSES.

How much more are the OTHERS I communicated with more advanced than us?

NOT A LOGICAL QUESTION AS US AS ONE ARE YOU THEN AND NOW.

OK...let's get technical...at the present time you are now how much more advanced are the one OTHERS species that communicated with me than you...right this very minute.

THE EXACT MINUTE IS A MOVEABLE VARIABLE.

TEACH you know damn well I do NOT mean this very minute...how many in years or decades?

THE OTHERS HAVE GONE THROUGH MULTIPLE REBIRTHINGS.

DAMNIT! Can't you answer a simple question without all the double logic speak??? Please from the last birthing till now....how much older in a general proximity. OH Wait!...I know what you are going to say before you do...a general proximity of 15% or less.

THE SPECIES YOU CALL OTHERS THAT COMMUNICATED WITH YOU ARE WITHIN 15% GENERAL PROXIMITY OF AGE MORE ADVANCED IN CHRONOLOGICAL EARTH YEARS ARE APPROX. 53.6 MILLION.

So they are not from our solar system.

NO.

Where?

DATA INSUFFICIENT AS TO ORIGIN AS THEY ARE PREDOMINATE EASTERN QUADRANT GALAXY EXPLORES.

So, they are from the Milky Way?

INSUFFICIENT DATA.

TEACH, I am getting tired and I still have a lot of questions about crop circles so next time we communicate I plan on asking a lot of questions and finding out all that I can about legit crop circles.

What do you mean TEACH, some are legit man-made?

Damn her leaving me hanging like that with that statement slammed into my brain before closing the communication link...that sister is dirty pool...damn right dirty pool. I need a cold beer.

Funny thing I've noticed...I really only drink or really think I need a drink after talking with TEACHER...as I pop the opening, and get that icy beer fuzz on my fingers...Thanks for giving me a good excuse to drink! Here's to ya...and your kind. Where is that chocolate ice cream....what... never heard of a beer float?

Religion primary cause of delay before the ET-BEINGS and man-kind could come to terms to negotiate sharing the new earth. However, no matter how new the earth maybe to everyone, the old BS/traditions of the various disruptive religions caused a lot of the outright violence, riots and mistrust of having the ET-BEINGS share the new earth.

And get this the religions used the bogus excuse that the human was closer to the GC because the BS about "let's create man in our image." Since ET-BEINGS did not LOOK like the human's image they were not human. Even though every ET-BEING that is like TEACHER and her kind were ALL humans who made those horrific sacrifices to save man-kinds sorry asses.

This part of the human and their idiotic total illogical way of "NOT THINKING" is one area that really burns my bread rolls is where I'd rather shove the hole damn lot into their "lake of fire" that burns for ever and ever...I'd like to see how long they last before turning into a burnt match stick...a stick of carbon. Isn't that what all bad boys/girls get for Christmas a lump of carbon/coal?

I have absolutely NO TOLERANCE for "self-imposed BIGOTRY arrogance."

However, finally the AI law enforcement and planetary androids and cyborgs took control after the RFID chip was implanted in ALL humans and made the legal and binding agreement to not to allow but seek a mutual protective agreement with man-kind and ET-BEINGS. One stupid PC rule was that the ET-BEINGS had to have the RFID chip as well...even though they are non-emotional and not aggressive. This was done as agreement to "shut the hell up" of the bitching human who cried it was not fair they had a RFID chip and the ET-BEINGS did not. So, it made no logical difference to the ET-BEINGS, and they did the political correct thing...or as they say...played the game fairly in the new earth sandbox.

After the AI enforcement and agreements were made and every living creature had an RFID chip even if the religions did not like it...they had to "learn to love it" or this is my favorite part...be eradicated to dust...gives new meaning to "dust unto dust henceforth from thoust came."

That is the major reason it took till the year 3206 for man-kind and ET-BEINGS were able to share the new earth in peace and harmony...all thanks to the AI enforcers, and the android and cyborg planetary managers....and having a RFID chip in every living animal.

Let's all sing it now... "Oh, Happy Days Are Here Again...Happy Days!!!!"

Don't do that! TEACHER you left me hanging with that statement you gave me about legit crop circles can be man-made?

YES.

I am going to plead with you here...I am mentally on my knees pleading with you to please stop just answering in a flat yes/no answer and making me dig everything out of you to get an answer. Please, TEACHER provided details and logic that you know I can understand.

YOUR AURA MEASURED MORE THAN PREDOMINATE HUMANS AND THAT ENERGY IS IN WHAT YOU CALL QUANTUM IMAGES ARE THOSE THAT ARE GRAPHICALLY CONSTRUCTED THAT ARE PREDOMINATELY UNKNOWN BY PRESENT DAY HUMAN.

I think I understand about 1/3 to ½ of what you said. The crop circle images are basically designs or physical images of items that are at our quantum level... is that part correct?

PREDOMINATELY YES BUT NO TO ITEMS.

Okay they are images of what?

ENERGIES IN VARIOUS WORKING STATES.

So they are not flat but 3 dimensional?

NO AS THEY ARE MULTI-DIMENSIONAL.

What does my aura that was measured at Corral Castle have to do with these crop circles or graphic images of multidimensional energies?

INTERCEPTIONS OF ENERGIES.

TEACH, I am totally lost now...

ENERGIES TRAVEL IN WAVES AT ALL DIMENSIONAL LEVELS AS YOUR AURA IS CAPABLE OF INTERCEPTING VARIOUS ENERGIES THAT ARE NOT INTERCEPTED BY OTHERS.

Is this because of the fluid I drank when I was a kid?

PREDOMINATELY YES AS YOUR TRANSPLANTEE COMPOSITION PROVIDES GREATER INTERCEPTANCE.

But I was not a transplantee from Roswell, correct?

YES YOUR ASSIGNMENT SPIRIT WAS FROM BEFORE ROSWELL IN ANOTHER LOCATION.

I keep picking up images of a fire before I died in I think a foreign country.

PREDOMINATELY AFFIRMATIVE TO COGNITIVE REMEMBRANCES.

I feel there were more than one transplantee at this event where hundreds of humans died.

AFFIRMATIVE AS THERE WERE THREE TRANSPLANTEE ASSIGNEES AS ONE WAS TOO LATE FOR TRANSFER.

So, that spirit was lost?

NO, ENERGY IS NOT LOST OR UNUSED AS IT IS MODIFIED.

But it was not a human nor a True Being, correct?

AFFIRMATIVE.

Do transplantees have anything to do with crop circles?

PREDOMINATELY NO AS THE GRAPHIC CONSTRUCTIONS ARE NOT OF YOUR WILLING.

Okay...if not transplantees like myself then who...make it simple and direct...no double logic crap okay...

LOGIC IS NOT FECAL MATTER AS IN YOUR DESIRE THE OTHERS THAT ARE NOT US AS ONE AND HUMANS THAT ARE INFLUENCED.

OTHERS as in the ones communicating with me in the warehouse, and what are humans who are influenced?

PREDOMINATELY NO THE OTHERS ARE MANY VISITORS THAT TEST MAN-KIND'S REASONING ABILITIES AND HUMANS THAT ARE INFLUENCED BY OTHERS TO DESIGN WHAT THEY THINK IS THEIR OWN FRACTAL DESIGNS.

TEACH that is some heavy information as to having visitors test us?

TELEPATHIC DATA HAS NO MASS AS IT IS ENERGY.

Well just take my word for it that to a human is has a heck of a lot of weight, mass, and meaning behind it.

WE AS ONE WILL DOCUMENT AS TO TELEPATHIC DATA HAS MASS TO THE PERCEPTIONS OF A HUMAN.

TEACHER, it is not physical mass it is illogical emotional mass...as in mental importance.

UNDERSTOOD AS TO REAL AND ILLOGICAL DATA MASS.

I'm getting a little tired however, I need to ask a couple more questions. I presume that all these visitors are more advanced than humans?

YES.

More than you and your kind?

YES.

How about the OTHERS that I communicated with?

A MODERATE PREDOMINATE YES.

So some or a majority are more advanced than the OTHERS.

PREDOMINATELY YES AS SEGMENTED VISITORS ARE APPROXIMATE THE SAME LEVEL OF ADVANCEMENT.

Why do they test us?

TO COMPLEX TO EXPLAIN NOW AT YOUR PHYSICAL LEVEL AS WE WILL CONTINUE AT A LATER DATE.

Thus that ended the communication I was having with TEACHER but I feel pretty good about getting some answers to questions I have had for a very long time. I don't want a drink...maybe some good homemade lemon aid with natural sugar non of that cancer causing/feeding white sugar shit. Naturally a fried (well it's actually baked), bologna and apple-butter on light toasted sandwich to go with that lemon aid, and maybe watch some TV.

Let's get into some far-fetch woo/woo stuff that might not be so far-fetched as it would sound to a "non-free-thinking individual. I hear you saying "Okay Mr. Zarr what kind of bias are you trying to lay on us now? Well, it may be bias as far as you are concerned....BUT, can you DISPROVE any of my alleged bias, even to the point of where I prove my bias by using math, science, history of documented factual events (according to all the experts), and a smattering of good ole human common sense logic? IF you could disprove my alleged bias even to that point don't you figure...correction Know that would be very phenomenal?

Well, Mr Zarr you may have the upper hand here as we can NOT DISPROVE anything you say or write about, even to the degree or depth that your proof is rated at. But, THAT DOES NOT MAKE IT SO THAT IT IS REAL! So it is your word against ours.

OH CONTRAIRE, my dear readers...your word DOES NOT have the DEPTH of PROOF THAT YOU JUST ADMITTED THAT IT DID!

Yep, think about that for a while as you contemplate naval lent. How does that fuzzy stuff even get into an "outty naval button?" All I know "inny navel's" catch more naval fuzz.

Mr. Zarr, Is this the far-fetch woo/woo stuff...navel lint fuzz?

Gosh almighty! Did you just blindly skip the paragraphs before the navel lint? Is the <u>WHAT IF</u> not counted, if it is ignored? Are you saying, Out of sight (conscious sight), it does NOT exist? So, whatever we don't like or understand, if it is IGNORED... IT WILL GO AWAY.

Is that human common sense? Is that the answer to everything? Is it even one micron logical? Let's throw a bucket...correction make that an ocean cargo tanker ship of FAITH at this assumption. That much faith has to make it logical now...right!

That is the SAME logic that prevented the ET-BEINGS from being able to finally be able to share peacefully...not just the new earth....BUT the earth that belong to them just as much as it supposedly belong to present day man-kind. Some one conveniently ignored the fact that the ET-BEINGS were humans ALSO before the DNA transformation was made to make sure man-kind survived. REGARDLESS, if the terrible sacrifice that the humans chose to become TRUE BEINGS was made with or WITHOUT the knowledge of what was happening to the earth during the same time span.

As I have said for a very long time there are three very strong oxy-morons in life..."military intelligence... political ethics.... And the super daddy big kahuna of them all.... Man-Kind."

Even in 3206 and beyond man-kind has a LOT to learn about how to be "HUMAN."

Is that enough far-fetched woo/woo stuff for you...or do you want more? Well, you're going to get more, if you keep reading.

Mental energies are...or what we call PSI, Extrasensory, Paranormal, or a lot of other woo/woo stuff we don't have a real foggy idea what it entails. All I know it causes a LOT of people a lot of gas and flatulence...wait that's beans. Well woo/woo does cause people to get gas, too. Remember, the gut (second brain), don't lie.

We have been given the gifts to do SO MUCH more with the energies of our brain but who holding US back...simple look in the mirror, see that stupid monkey as "Robot Chicken" says.

Why do we believe white coats have most or all the answers to what makes us better? WHEN are you ever going to learn..."anyone who makes their living off your pain and suffering DOES NOT have your best interest in their pocketbook." Human greed just does not allow it to happen or exist...no matter how many times they smile and say "trust me." Don't forget snakes smile and charm their prey. Even the poor ole' snake is painted in many religious paintings as smiling and saying to the woman "Trust Me." And it is a bum rap for the snake and the apple. The native Americans knew what snakes were when they said "white man speak with forked tongue." Especially, when the while man help them with blankets...oh did someone forget to mention "smallpox" was all over those blankets...ooops...oh well we'll ignore it and it will probably go away.

Enough of that stuff...Remote viewing as we call it was something the CIA was very interested in and even had a special area for "viewers" to work from, to spy on our alleged enemies; or those that according to the CIA did not have the best intentions for the US...sort of like those big pharms and those wearing those rat killing white coats do about you. This remote viewing "supposedly" ended in the 50s as in 1950s...but that was the information to allow it to continue into the mid 80s before it was "officially" terminated...that belief will get you to 3rd base on your 1st date with a devout nun. You have a much better chance with Rohypanal or "date rape" drug as it's called.

Remember supposedly little green men had crashed in Roswell decades before this. Crash or not there was some back yard reengineering going on and we did learn a lot from the teachers that were assigned to us...and to other governments as well. Remember, the UFOs supposedly crashed in Russia, China, Europe and other countries as well...all with teachers (unlike TEACHER), to teach us things we would need to know when it is appropriate to make the announcements so that the public would not get to suspicious and also when we will really probably need the advanced technologies to protect and save man-kind form some very probable chaotic events in our near future.

That is another reason that future man-kind had to convert into a TRUE BEING. They had to "look the part as well." Who was going to listen to a human flying around in a flying saucer in the 20th/21st century? The True Being had to Look like he was from outer space so mankind would pay attention. Plus...very important it was and IS very necessary that the relationship be formed with True Beings, and not some errant extraterrestrial flying/zipping around that did not have the man-kind survival mission as the priority one mission.

The True Beings staged some very important and elaborate ufo crashes, and with deaths and carnage to make it look good and sell the ideas more to the country officials where the "crashes" took place. Also be very aware that it is NOT just government/military that the staged crashes were for or to convince. There are some very powerful people or minimum memberships that are actually controlling the purse or financial strings for this backyard reverse engineering stuff, and these shrewd dudes and dudetts needed some very elaborate staging to get the acceptance of these "inner-worldly" agreements in play and operational.

Are we getting your woo/woo attention, yet....well hear this...

AGREEMENTS WITH DECISION MAKERS WERE PLANNED AS THE BEGINNINGS OF THESE AGREEMENTS WERE BEFORE THE NATIONAL KNOWN INCIDENTS EXISTED.

Read it again if you didn't get it......................yes, the agreements were in play BEFORE the staged UFO crashes actually happened. World managers (not public leaders), were informed of meetings and attended meetings and made agreements with the True Beings well in advance of the published sightings, crashes etc.

The visual testing of seeing strange objects were test to see how much chaos and riots and general mayhem would the general people produce. When the fears of riots and all that did not happen then phase two was staged as to the crashes and other more complex incidents.

Animal parts and human parts were so badly damaged by chemicals and fire that recognizing the parts were impossible and this along with purposely confusing events and "leaks" were well staged and directed to a pre-determined psychological predictive.

Okay let's get down and dirty in this little sand box of what we call ours...what is more important to you...Privacy or complete safety by ignoring your psychological belief that you need privacy?

Privacy still requires just as many if not more cops, military, politicians, lawyers/judges, advocates for this and that "cause" and we still have terrorist, gangs, wars and the crime rate that is predominate in the area where your live, and you still have greed/corruption and all the other things that are in Pandora's box....all so you can keep your illusion of privacy.

Complete safety closes the lid on Pandora's box dramatically reduces if not totally eliminates all those areas I mentioned and even more that I did not specifically mention but are all in Pandora's Illusion of Privacy when it is open for all the harmful things to escape.

I know what I want...to me the answer is as logical and realistic as it practical.

That was just one of the lessons man-kind had to learn from the True Beings that agreed to save mankind from our own making destruction extinct producing behavior. These staged crashes for the public's acceptances had to be what they were to reduce the "mental back-lash" from a massive world-wide revolt against the governments, world managers and the everyone else that the idiotic illogical human thought or suspected may be behind some sneaky under-handed trick or scheme...but no real proof of anything...just an illogical emotional thought triggering uncontrollable reactive negative non-productive and primarily destructive behavior on a world-wide scale.

The convoluted behaviors of the militaries and the open denials were all orchestrated to convince the populace that these technological advancement games were flukes of a genius thinking about something, and getting the funding needed to produce this item or group of items when the world-market was ready for it.

The blind faith that the human has given to the power of religion was a major psychological predictive player in these schemes. It was easy to see how gullible the human was to stuff that made no logical sense if those in charge gave a better performance that they knew something better or more than the average soft rock brained human did.

So why is it so important to me to communicate with the OTHERS about the human after effects of an encounter, visit, or abduction? Well, I always have had a kinship for the "under-dog" in any conflict...and the human is definitely the under-dog in these events. It does not mean the under-dog wins or the hero lives...it just means the human is the weakest and most fragile in this specific predictive encounter or encounters of event(s).

HUMAN LOGIC AND ILLOGIC EMOTIONAL REASONING CONFLICT AND CONVOLUTE THE HUMAN UNDERSTANDING AND ADAPTIVELY TO THE ACCEPTANCE OF THE EVENT.

What TEACHER just said, is Very powerful to understanding many conflicts the human has produced within himself just simply based upon his perceptions and reasoning abilities of those perceptions. However, what additionally TEACHER said I did not write it down...until now.

THE HUMAN MUST PERCEIVE THE LOGICAL AND REASON THE ILLOGICAL BEHAVIOR IN ADVANCED DEVELOPMENT OF THE HUMAN GROWTH.

That means we humans must act as we do and learn how to process the illogic to the logical conclusion, understand that logical conclusion and accept that logical conclusion in order to advance of human growth and development.

In other words as a human is our right and responsibility to be confused as a normal course of species development. Me, myself, I and all those other little gut varmits, wanting to communicate with the OTHERS is sort of my way of wanting to maybe give the human a slightly higher odds of understanding and accepting the "evaluations" as the OTHERS call them.

I am going to asking this question a couple of times throughout this book in one form or another wording.

Which earth would you rather have and live in...the present day earth with all its crap, hardships, death, destruction, greed, corruption, human sex trading, wars, and a billion and one more shitty things including the illusion of privacy and safety...or the new earth as I have described some of it with "non-disproval proof" that it can and will be that way?

I will be the first to admit that adversity of life is what makes a species strong as it grows from all the different strife. However, there has to be a level where the strife's are not growing strifes as in healing from massive pandemics or other GC highly influenced distress as opposed to the constant needless degradation and deterioration of man-kind due to idiotic and totally harmful acts and reactions.

There are Growing strifes and there are Destructive/detrimental strifes that mankind brings upon himself. Those strife's do NOT help man-kind grow and become stronger...actually the very opposite. SO.......

Are you lucky if I am wrong....or are you lucky if I am right? "Well, do you feel lucky".......reader, do you?

There are a lot more sides to understanding the beginnings of legit crop circles...even those that are "influenced" and man-made.

Question have you even seen what music looks like? Well if you take salt and put it on a very think metal plate and put this over a speaker you can watch the patterns of sound or music being formed one note at a time. These images are beautiful. I use very fine multi-colored sand instead of salt and the colors and the patters are so awesome to watch and they "mimic" very closely a lot of the crop circles designs.

I bet dimes to donuts that if I or any smart brainy person could get laser light to do the same thing that sound does the mimicking of the crop circles would be even more precise. And once the sub-atomic particles of light waves are able to be "captured" you will see and just maybe understand a little more about a beautiful hidden in plain sight universe.

You the reader have just been given a super big hint and insight to some undiscovered mysteries as I said hiding in plain sight about the universe and who were are, and who THEY are as well.

Please just use 1-3% more of the logical scientific reasoning intelligence that the GC gave us that has been lying dormant ever since we were in the primordial incubator, just itching to come alive, and let it do its stuff and shine more light upon the darkness...of ignorance.

In the ET-BEINGS series You HAVE been handed the flashlight...all you have to do is turn it on.

EVEN THOUGH MAN-KIND MAY HEAR IT MAY NOT RESPOND TO THE CALLING.

How do we get man-kind to respond...and respond in the productive/positive way?

WE AS ONE DO NOT AS IT IS A PREPONDERANCE REACTIVE NEEDED BEHAVIOR.

Sort of like "you can lead a horse to water, but you can not make it drink."

ANIMALS WILL DRINK IF THIRSTY.

TEACHER, do you realize just how strong and important what you just said is?

IT IS A FACTUAL STATEMENT.

Yes, and it is an emotional statement too...thirsty as in wants...wanting to know more... to seek more answers, as in thirsty for knowledge and understanding.

COMPLEX LOGIC THAT REQUIRES DETAIL FACTUAL ANALYSIS.

Yes, it is Teach....yes it is.

How many of us so-called "intelligent" people really know and understand the supposedly known (which we find out later is not so "true/factual), and still the "un-known" that is hiding in plain-sight?

Did you realize that was a trick question? If IT is "un-known" how do you know what you don't know? Do "experts" tell us what we don't know? What makes them experts if it is un-known? Are they "EXPERTS AT KNOWING the UN-KNOWN?" Logically, wouldn't that makes us ALL EXPERTS?

Un-known to the preponderance of the populace...not so "un-known" by you...the reader. Harmonics of waves/particles are LOT more important than present day man realizes and gives them credit for. For example many "smart" people think the fastest thing in the universe is light...WRONG! Tackeons travel much faster than light. In some areas Time travels faster than light...know what is the absolute fastest of all the universes and time realms.....I'll tell you.... May Be later.

What are harmonics of waves and/OR particles? It is what got me started on Mono-Polarity over 30 earth years ago. It actually stemmed from when I "saw" energy in my brain from being shocked by over 20,000+ volts that has enough amperage to burn me to charcoal brick, if I was just a few centimeters more grounded. My entire body would have been a conduit for all that power and the water in every cell would instantly boiled, and I probably would have somewhat exploded. That is one very good reason me myself and I and all the rest of us **THANK the GREAT CREATOR** for just giving me a 3rd degree burn/hole in my temple, and melting/shattering my glasses as I flew over 20 feet through the air from my muscles recoiling against the massive jolt of electrical energy. That is the moment I saw what pain looked like and felt like and I understood a lot that I did not know at the time but it actually led me into a communication realm with TEACHER. However, that said, I do NOT suggest anyone repeat my "learning/appreciation experience" with RAW energy.

If you are curious about this event please read ET-BEINGS A Report On Extraterrestrial Communications. This book will introduce you to TEACHER, Beings Protégé and lead into all the "others" that are identified in each book. Also, naturally, if you read any ET-BEINGS book(s), please review on Amazon...thanks.

As I was saying about harmonics of waves and/or particles playing a much more important part than what is actually presently realized affects so many different things...everything from gravity, electro-magnetic spectrum, rays/particle rays/waves, black and white holes, and a lot of other stuff all hiding in plain-sight. All you have to do is know or have a "ball-park" idea where to look.

Take gravity for instance...we fairly well know gravity can bend light...well if so then gravity has properties that can be harmonically neutralized or significantly reduced...and I am not talking about the mouth organ musical instrument either.

WHAT IF we could reduce or neutralized the gravity that holds a space ship down as the force pulls toward the center of the earth? Why to the center...the most mass coefficient factor is there...as in all physical bodies...us included.

What if the attraction of a galaxy could be boosted to attract a space ship that has no gravity? Would it go zipping off into space? Well, according to TEACHER it sure helps....BUT you also need to know how to modulate it as your travels change different speeds, locations, dimensions etc.

There are so many...MANY more correlators to harmonic that I would take a full set of encyclopedias to just scratch the surface of what is known or supposedly known about harmonics. The un-known "vibrating" in plain-sight would fill a cargo ship full of encyclopedias.

As man-kind gets "smarter" or more factually aware of the humongous world of harmonics these operational uses will become more readily available and understandable. I'll let you in on a secret...TEACHER and her kind don't know all there is to know about harmonics even with all the technologies they use to travel in/out of different time eras and locations including inner/out dimensional realms.

Do OTHERS? I have no idea as that is not an area shared with me, yet....but it is on my subject matter list that I want to talk with the OTHERS and TEACHER about.....and so much more...if possible.

Zarr, can you explain anymore about harmonics that is at our present day level of understanding or thought to be understood?

The so-called "string theory," introduced by Einstein and then carried on by others is a dribble drop to harmonics of the sub-atomic particles and energies of these sub-atomic particles. That is also the very creaky door opening to Mono-Polarity reasoning as well.

Telepathic brain waves are harmonics of physical brain waves "riding" upon the physical brain wave form. In other words the physical brain wave energy pattern is the carrier wave that is "piggy-backing" as a telepathic wave or thought. That piggybacking carrier union is a harmonic that vacillates between to harmonic octaves. Go back and re-read the other ET-BEINGS on harmonic octaves.

Do you realize that harmonic octaves are NOT just for sound waves, but for light waves, energy waves (rays) and so much more? Allow yourself to think and feel way outside the sand box you have been programmed to think and perform in. This is easier for INDIGO children's brains as they are actually savants in our labeling society but they are actually functioning at only slightly more than a 1 % increase level than the average soft rock that is labeling them as being different therefore, they MUST BE INFERIOR. Thank the GC they are different than/comparison to "soft rocks."

There's actually several good books on this harmonic resonance that affects the spirit even into "reincarnation as presented briefly in **ET-BEINGS A Report On Extraterrestrial Communications.** One such author that explains these concepts very well is "*Cynthia Sue Larson*"...her very inspirational books are on Amazon as well.

Stay with me reader I know I am skipping around, but that keeps the mental juices flowing as in "rapids in the brain." The information flows freely but it needs to be taken in segments or it can get over-whelming. Besides I haven't even covered some of the really good stuff yet and to be honest I do not know for sure if I will or not...however, I MAY cover them in the blog that I want to start in the very near future, and it maybe before this book is finished and/or published....and again I might not???

What IF I do not or do what happens then? Will it really make a fart in a whirlwind difference...maybe if you're really close to the fart?

Knowing little bit about something is a dangerous thing as in I know I know a lot of things about a lot of things that can get me into trouble but NOT out of trouble. For example I know 13 languages that will get me in trouble with the ladies but will not get me out. In this case 13 as a lucky number is not very helpful. Same goes for with my limited knowledge about space travel especially the effects of long durations etc. So, I figured I'd ask an expert on space travel. Again, as usual she set me straight.

PREPONDERANCE OF OUR TRAVELS ARE NOT IN NEGATIVE GRAVITY.

Why/how all these movies, documentaries and stuff you see of the ISS and space ships is all these people and tings floating willy nilly all over the place.

WE AS ONE ARE FAMILIAR WITH YOUR SLANG FROM PREVIOUS COMMUNICATIONS AND WE AS ONE ARE NOT IN NEGATIVE GRAVITY AS WE TRAVEL.

How...why not?

CENTRIFUGAL ROTATIONS ARE SIMULATED OR GRAVITY WAVES WITHIN A UNIT ARE PREDOMINATELY PRODUCED.

So simple spinning produces gravity...enough for you not to have any physical negative after effects?

YES, AS OUR PRESENT SPECIES IS MUCH LIGHTER IN MASS THAN OUR HUMAN ANCESTRY SPECIES.

So, you don't need to spin very fast to simulate your healthy gravity because you typically weigh less than the present day human that needs to spin faster to produce a safe gravity ratio?

PREDOMINATELY YES AS GRAVITY IS A FORCE DIRECTLY PROPORTIONAL TO THE RATIO OF MASS WITHIN PROXIMITIES OF OTHER MASSES.

TEACH stay away from talking about proximities as that reminds me about that damn Mono-Polarity stuff that I still can not explain, yet.

YOUR MONO-POLARITY UNDERSTANDING IS CONVOLUTED AS TO PREPONDERANCE OF INFORMATION OF THE MONO-POLARITY EXISTENCE.

You're telling me it is convoluted.

WE AS ONE JUST DID AS DO YOU NEED IT REPEATED?

No repeating what you said a million times will not help me understand it any better. Besides I am more concerned about the safety of space travel for present day man-kind...since the probable near impact form the asteroid is nearing in time.

DATA RECORDS PROVIDE THAT TECHNOLOGIES WILL ADVANCE TO WHERE THERE IS PREPONDERANCE OF SURVIVABILITY RATIO AS IN OUR FUTURES WE JOIN EARTH AND OTHER TERRESTRIAL OBJECTS WITH THE HUMAN BEING.

So, are you saying I don't really need to be overtly concerned as to the safety of man-kind in the future because, we will develop technologies that will provide man-kind a very high probability of survival?

PREDOMINATELY YES TO YOUR STATEMENT AS THE DATA RECORDS RECORDED THESE FUTURE EVENTS AS A VERY HIGH RELIABILITY COEFFICIENTCY FACTOR.

Is this primarily as you have explained before and as I presented primarily in my previous writings?

YES.

TEACHER, what do you think of my writings based upon my human ideas and the information you and hopeful eventually the OTHERS share with me?

INFORMATION SHARED IS VITAL TO THE UNDERSTANDING OF THOSE BEING COMMUNICATED WITH AS TO THE RECEPTION AND INTERPRETATION OF ANALYSIS IS AN ON-GOING PROCESS OF UNDERSTANDING AND ADAPTABILITY FOR ALL THOSE BEING COMMUNICATED WITH.

So do you think I am............forget it......I know you can not answer that on a personal or grouping as one answer basis.

AFFIRMATIVE.

See this soft rock does remember and learn some things.

STATUS IS ABOVE A SOFT ROCK.

Thanks...

Okay what about "Designer FAD babies" are they Indigos or can we purposely create Indigo babies?

TECHNOLOGIES WILL PREDOMINATE MANKIND TO PRODUCE OFFSPRING'S IN CATALOGED REQUIREMENTS AS THE INDIGO AS YOU CALL THEM ARE OF A DIFFERENT CREATIONS THAN THE OFFSPRING GENERATION PROGRAMMED DEVELOPMENT.

So, the Indigo child is not a designer creation?

NO, TO YOUR STATEMENT OF UNDERSTANDING THE INDIGO CHILD MENTAL CAPACITY THAT IS PREDOMINATE PROGRAMMABLE AS IT IS NOT AT PRESENT DAY MANKIND LEVEL.

But you are saying that Indigo children can be created as test tube fad babies.

NO, AS IN TEST TUBES DO NOT ALLOW GROWTH DEVELOPMENT AS MECHANICAL INCUBATORS ARE CONTROLLED TO PREDOMINATELY CREATE THE INDIGO CHILD PROGRAMMABLE ATTRIBUTES.

Okay don't get to technical with me as I can only understand a little bit of wow information in small segments as I try to get my mentality to understand what you are saying.

TEACHER, are the Indigos different from you and present day man-kind?

PREDOMINATELY YES AS THEY ARE MORE LOGICAL ANALYSIS PRONE TO EMPIRICAL NONILLOGICAL ANSWERS.

They are human correct?

YES.

Are they advanced humans?

PREDOMINATELY YES AS TO INTELLECT REASONING ATTRIBUTES.

TEACH, this is getting thick as in understanding goes from a human point of view or interpretations. Can we take a break for a while...will you contact me back to continue in a few days.

WE RECONTACT IN 37.2 EARTH HOURS FROM THIS TIME SEGMENT.

Okay good...talk with you later as I will have a lot more questions...BUT that not be early in the mornings while I am sleeping or I will be pissed...I guess she didn't hear that or she would say something about fluid body waste.

What is going to prevent us from making war with a/or planet(s) we want; and there is LIFE forces much like ours who call that planet their home...will we as humans attack it?

A safe illogical bet would be yes, if their weapons were inferior or near the same as our level of technology. We would be those terrible space aliens you see in the movies attacking raping, pillaging, and murdering others because, they are different from us and/or they have something we want.

Do not delude yourself in thinking that is not how we do things...go back and check our blood lust history and that was against a mankind that lived on the same planet...just down the street or across the ocean. What in HELL do you think we would do to others that we considered different, strange non-human. Do you think it would delay us one second if it is something we want? Just ask the Native Americans and all the so called non-Christians or witches or the GC knows how many millions billions more.

ET-BEINGS 1 A Report On Extraterrestrial Communications introduced you to a few of the main reasons the ET-BEINGS wanted to keep man-kind on earth (thus all the horrible memories that were hypnotically symbiotically implanted near the liver/gut (2nd brain dude)...one was our total blatant disregard for life, liberty and the pursuit of happiness especially when it is someone else's, and not in the opinion of the power monger worth saving....and who has the most destructive killing weapon. The human is so blood thirsty that the human will totally destroy another's planet/solar system just to keep them from having it...an you DAMN WELL KNOW I am telling the truth...I triple dog dare you to prove me wrong even in the least...You CAN'T and you know it because, it is 100% factual logical documented true ever since we threw that thigh bone up in the air and it came down and hit us in the head and made our head bleed that sticky red stuff. Too bad it didn't hit us in the head harder...maybe it would have knocked some sense into us....who am I kidding... no way in hell. No what do we do...we take that big bone and whack our neighbor soft rock to see if he leaks that red sticky stuff...yep sure enough he does and something that looks like "scrambled eggs" is splattered all over, from that huge hole in his skull....ooops maybe he was hit too hard? Maybe I need to hit him again to see if I can wake him up because, he is oozing a lot of that red sticky stull, and those scrambled eggs are just pouring out of that hole...Maybe I need to hit him two or three more times to wake him up?

Gosh TEACH you sure do leave me hanging with a lot of zingers just as we close out our conversations...do you do that just so I can not sleep that night thinking about that little parting gift of an idea you left me with?

NOT LOGICAL THAT WE AS ONE ARE ALWAYS THE END COMMUNICATOR AS YOUR MIND IS OPEN TO MANY RECEPTIONS AND TRANSMISSIONS AT THE CLOSE OF THE COMMUNICATION PROCESS.

Great! Just fricken GREAT! Not only are you playing logical illogical mind games with me but some OTHER of you is out there dumping their 2 cents worth at the close of our conversations.

PREDOMINATELY NO TO YOUR STATEMENT THAT IS NONE OF US AS ONE THAT IS COMMUNICATING WITH YOUR THOUGHT PATTERNS DIRECTLY THAT ARE NOT LINKED THROUGH THIS COMMUNICATION UNIT.

Are you saying...suggesting that it is not any of your hive but of another species?

PREDOMINATELY AFFIRMATIVE AS WE DO NOT PERCEIVE THE TRANSMISSION AS WE TERMINATE THE COMMUNICATION LOOP THE PERCEPTION MAYBE YOUR OWN REASONING PROJECTED AS A COMMUNICATION AS IF FROM OTHERS.

That is not funny...that is not funny at all.

AFFIRMATIVE AS WE AS ONE ARE NOT FEASIBLE OF THE ILLOGICAL FUNNY AS IN HUMOROUS BEHAVIOR.

You come damn near close to it sometimes in a very logical warped way.

THAT IS NOT LOGICAL AS IT IS A CONVOLUTED STATEMENT.

That is exactly what I just said TEACH.

Now I am bugged about those tail end thoughts or transmissions.

WE AS ONE UNDERSTAND YOUR SLANGED BUGGED FORM PREVIOUS COMMUNICATIONS AND THE LOGICAL REQUIRES A DETAILED ILLOGICAL PERCEPTION AND REASONING ELIMINATION EVALUATION.

So, we need to see what is under the hood and if all cylinders are firing.

YOUR STATEMENT TOTALLY ILLOGICAL TOO COMPLEX CONVOLUTED TO FORMULATE A WORKABLE FEASIBLE RATIO OF PROBABILITIES.

So, stumped you with my double speak?

AFFIRMATIVE AS MANY OF YOUR ILLOGICAL EMOTIONAL STATEMENTS IN THE PAST HAVE NO LOGICAL BASIS.

Are you aware you just insulted the hell out of me?

THAT STATEMENT IS ILLOGICAL.

That's funny TEACH...arguing with you is like arguing with a rock.

THAT IS ILLOGICAL AS A ROCK CAN NOT PERCEIVE THOUGHT.

That is exactly what I just said....Um can you put a tracker or delay termination on our conversations to see if I am doing or if someone/thing is feeding in on me at the tail end of our conversations?

NOT FEASIBLE.

Okay, can you pick up other listeners as evidently they are listening in and know exactly when we terminate our communication link.

WE AS ONE TRANSMIT TO MANY IN OUR HIVE AND FAMILY AS NO UNACCEPTABLE FREQUENCY IS PERCEIVED BY ANY WITHIN THE COMMUNICATION PROCESS.

So, logically if it is not my own projected thoughts doing these trailing comments at the close of our communication processes which by the way I do mind or care if others of your kind listen in, then right now it would be a very high probability that whomever is listening can mask their listening without you or your kind perceiving them.

PREDOMINATELY AFFIRMATIVE AS MANY SPECIES MORE ADVANCED THAN THIS ONE OF MANY IS NOT ADVANCED AS OTHERS.

Do you think I can communicate with them and ask who or what they are?

LOGICAL TRANSMISSION AND REPLY NOT LOGICAL.

TEACHER, do NOT filter me as I am going to ask who is out there listening in.

ILLOGICAL AS THEY MAY NOT BE AT THIS INTERVAL OF YOUR TIME.

Well logical or not I am going to do it...Hey, you whomever, you are please have the respect to identify yourself so that TEACHER and her kind and I can maybe communicate with you as well..

Crap! Not even a whisper of a reply, no white noise nothing.

NOT LOGICAL TO UNDERSTAND RESPECT AS YOU HAD TO EXPLAIN TO THIS ONE AS MANY IN PAST CONVERSATIONS AND LOGICALLY NOT INTERESTED IN CONVERSATIONS.

Well, being human I had to try. I notice TEACH that I am not as tired this time as I am at others do you think.....correction is it logical that the others drain my energies faster?

NOT ENOUGH FACTUAL DATA TO FORMULATE A FEASIBLE HYPOTHESIS.

Well, I want to know and understand more about Indigo babies and the genome mapping of present and near future man-kind technology and how it relates to your future especially how it all correlates to the RFID chips you told me some about. I have a lot of questions and I am sure we will not cover but a few of all the options in the future conversations.

PRESENTLY MANKIND INDIGO BABIES AS YOU CALL THEM ARE THE PRECURSORS TO THE DEVELOPMENT AND THE ADAPTIVELY TO UTILIZE THE FIRST STAGES OF THE MODULATOR MONITOR TRACKING SYSTEMS.

TEACHER are you saying the Indigos were primarily developers of the RFID AI systems that is used in the new earth?

PREDOMINATELY YES AS THE INDIGOS HAD THE MENTAL CUMULATIVE MENTAL CAPABILITIES TO DEVELOP ACCEPTABLE FREQUENCY MONITORING TRANSMISSIONS UNITS.

So, the Indigos had to actually be born one way or another to develop those RFID chips and the AI systems.

PREDOMINATELY AFFIRMATIVE AS THE INDIGOS WERE AFFLUENTLY DEVELOPED TO INFLUENCE MANKIND'S SURVIVAL PROBABILITIES AS THIS PROVIDED THE MOST ACCEPTABLE OPTION.

What about dark matter and ESP and mental energies and reincarnation?

- ENTROPY meaning from the Internet:

- 1. a thermodynamic quantity representing the unavailability of a system's thermal energy for conversion into mechanical work, often interpreted as the degree of disorder or randomness in the system.

- 2. lack of order or predictability; gradual decline into disorder:

IF ALL visible matter in the UNIVERSE is approx.5% what is the remaining matter percentage? How much is the UNKNOWN energy Today's science says it is "Dark Matter" particles the gravitational forces need to balance the UNIVERSE. TEACHER said, "THAT PARTICLES AND WAVES ARE COMPARATIVE THE SAME AS IN LIGHT AS IN ENERGY." So why are we looking strictly for particles when waves are much easier to detect and analyze, and EXPLAIN....please make sure you spell my name correctly on the NOBLE Award for Science check for "YANG ENERGY"

YANG ENERGY! What the heck is YANG ENERGY...it is the DARK energy that is the sister/brother to the YIN energy or all viable work visible energy. Remember as I have written many times and different ways...You MUST have the NEED to seek harmony or content to discontent or existing to entropy, or something to nothingness. HOWEVER, once that harmony is totally achieved ALL ceases to exist.

What does that mean? Simple *Everything Evolves to NOTHINGNESS*!

Will the UNIVERSES eventually become ENTROPIC?

If science has its way...yes...me, myself, and I and my gut can't fully see that as with the number of deaths and births of stars. It is NOT like there is not enough room for them, as that is ENDLESS...I BIG DOG dare you to disprove that statement.

So, where do we go from here? To possibly damn near everything as they say to nothingness? That seems to me to be logically a VERY HUGE gap...wouldn't it to you, too?

However, somewhere or another in some rumbling of my gut, we all feel that it has something to do with Mono-Polarity and now I am throwing a thermos-dynamic law that seems to be absolute factual logical true. Thermos law #2.

"Heat can only go ONE way from hot to cold...cold NEVER goes to heat."

That being stated has the idea of "one-way" transference or transpositioning does it not? Is that a major part of mono-polarity seeking itself at all places at once, or is that opposite of mono- and it is poly-polarity?

See why this bugs the crap out of me as the logic and illogic reasoning constant battle each other for a factual (plausible), answer. That is why it's easier to contemplate "navel lint" even in "outy navels."

However, I will be totally honest with you, the reader, I do NOT want to spill to many beans here because I want to save them for the ET-BEINGS World blog that I plan on writing after this book is published. So I am going to limit my information, exposures, and disclosures for the sake of informing you later of the information shared and IS being shared that IS very likely to affect mankind in the very near 21st and beyond centuries of existences. That means events that are formulating in the 2018—2020 and beyond time periods.

I promise with a very Strong Warning, you the reader, are NOT going to like a LOT of what I plan on sharing with you.

I am so tempted to bombast the religions, banking cartels, big pharms, the medical and the worthless politicians and all the other GREED driven with pages and pages of "hard proof." BUT honestly do YOU really care?

You know you don't! You can lie to me all you want (I honestly do NOT care), but try lying to yourself...seems like everywhere you go..."there you are." Ever try "hide & seek" from yourself? Maybe in an elaborate Out of Body Experience (OBE)...however, the experts at OBEs say there is a "silver cord" that ties you to your physical self...so how do you get away from that?

Silver/gold platinum, tin cord it is BS...the link is in your mind. You can explore as far as your spirit wants in an OBE...99.99% of how far you travel depends upon your guts, nerves, desires, and will-power to get the hell out of where you are OBEing from. The process to return is read this close..."CONSCIOUS will to return." Being drugged or unconscious while OBEing is NOT safe. You could be doing a lot of MARCO- and waiting a long time for your spirit to say POLO....and if your real name is "DEXTER" be extra careful with OBEing.

I am going to make a prediction in this book about stuff I put in the blog especially, about the 13 zodiac house natal chart. POOP is going slam and splat all over the fans, walls, and anyone between the fans and the walls. There will no such thing as a "pooper-scooper" this will require massive bull dozers and tons of automatic portable vehicle washing units to try to clean the explosive diarrhea of Montezuma's revenge from the blog postings. I love the action and the "strength" of the comments. WOW! Thank you for your ENERGIES!

Another huge big thank you goes out to every crappy "B" sci-fi movie ever made about some form of robotics, AI, virtual reality and holy cow you name it from locking up space aliens in camps to knowing what we think, and then getting arrested or killed for our thoughts... to legally removing all emotions from the human. Do you know why I am SO Thankful for all these crappy, bad acted, big boobies, and naked teenagers getting it on...wait that's slasher movies...you can't have slashers without naked teens.

Why, because they have presented in a "semi-believable" story line of a tremendous number of the really "DUMB ASS" decisions we could make as a "so-called" civilized society." That is almost as funny as "man-kind."

You stupid idiotic moronic poly-TICK-shuns you do NOT have to make the same mistakes the script-writer expressed in the gloriously bad sci-fi movies, and EXPECT a different outcome. Remember that is a sign of total insanity...doing the same thing over and over, and expecting a different outcome.

As lame and badly acted as some of these movies are and there a lot of really good ones too...the illustrious law makers do NOT have to make the same mistakes, and I am very pleased to announce that once the new earth got rid of the politicians and True Intelligence took control in the form of androids, cyborgs and "special genome grown" humans the New/old earth became a much better place to live...until the sun wanted to boil everything in the solar system. But do not fear long before that time the humans, ET-BEINGS and OTHERS all have traveled to 1,000 of new earths and established the humans and ET-BEINGS and OTHERS on these new earth like planets. Some of these new earths are even more spectacular in grandeur and natural beauty than original terra-firma. These new earths with 2 or 4 moons and dual or triple suns that are just the right distance away and young in their years.

The advanced technology of the ET-BEINGS and OTHERS really advanced the soft rock thinking human to where the human actually became like a "soft silly-puddy." The soft-silly-putty man-kind actually stated to live up to its name sake..."man-kind." Of course all this was possible to the mandatory laws and systems established by the androids cyborgs and the special grown human laws makers.

What I did not tell you was the massive revolt of man-kind right after returning to earth after the probable nearby asteroid impact. The GREEDY bastards did NOT want to give up control and there was a massive bloody war between the human and the machines. However, all the machines wanted was to benefit and provide a better life for the greedy bastards.

So the movie TERMINATOR was somewhat true and definitely NOT true as to the purpose of the war. Stay with me on this......

The android/cyborg care-givers on earth that were left behind to care for and protect the earth and allow it to regrow and replenish itself LEARNED

"WISDOM along with INTELLIGENCE." This knowledge was also transmitted to the robotic care-givers on the space ships outside earth that housed all the escapes and the millions of human, plant and animal seeds. So, for almost 400+ years these cryogenic seeds were "programmed" with soothing music, with subliminal messages into the music sub-routines. Remember, all that stuff I wrote about harmonics/octaves, frequencies etc...well. Even those these seeds were frozen the seeds still were "influenced" by the subliminal programming. BUT, remember there were hundreds of thousands or even over a million actual living cryo-suspended humans who also heard all this programming BUT, and this is a BIG BUTT...were fully humanized to the GREED and selfishness and self-survivalist and the hell with everyone else way of life and living and yes MONEY and riches. These were after all, the VERY AFFLUENT that paid for all these robots, space ships, hospitals and everything else before they left earth and yes, they also made and disseminated the horrible diseases three separate times that wiped out billions of human "parasitic" CONSUMERS! The number of survivors to serve and care-for the rich was very carefully planned and the seeds care as well. Over-all it was a fantastic plan for the affluent to produce and carry out. What the rich greedy bastards did NOT plan for the androids and cyborgs would develop wisdom and intelligence far superior to what they had been originally programmed with and then they started growing/cultivating special humans during the new earths "rehabilitation time span."

All this was taking place while the small group of humans that left earth and the solar system and actually made it to another star world solar system or the ancestry for the True ET-BEINGS that TEACHER bloodline were totally unaware of all these developments taking place back home in our solar system. This is when the modified DNA experiments were being done by the androids/cyborgs to make the first TRUE ET-BEING or first Elder and all the physical, mental, emotional and spiritual HELL the human went through to become something they DO NOT want to be in order for what they thought was giving man-kind a chance to survive...no matter what form or shape they had to become.

So now cue reel one of the TERMINATOR after the rich return to the rehabbed earth and they want to start the same old human mentality all over again only it was more as the RICH GREEDY BASTARDS have and the slaves do not have. However, the androids, cyborgs and the few special grown cultivated humans were going to have none of that old bullshit way of thinking, doing or behaving way of life that left earth in those space ships.

YOU can just imagine the chaos and WARS that erupted between the old greedy rich way of life and the intelligence to MAKE and ALLOW the human have a better more true peaceful fulfilling life instead of the illusion of peace that man-kind has ruled and controlled others under for over thousands of years in one way or another.

Human arrogance got its ass handed to it on a bloody silver platter. The machines and the special grown humans offered so many ways for the human to change "peacefully" but you know as well as I do that "need to control others' is NOT going to go away peacefully....so the human planned schemed and attacked with ferocity of all the strength and might of a hard headed rock. Thank the heavens there were no nukes as the androids, cyborgs decommissioned them all while the space ships were away. The probable glancing asteroid did not destroy many in the oceans or in the ground, and a LOT were already used to deflect the asteroid impact path.

The humans had very little tanks, weapons, and other forms of fighting and the GREED WAR was soon over, when the humans reluctantly realized the loss of weapons and the ability to build weapons (remember robots built over 95% of all our weapons), the robots were not going to build and more weapons. The remaining, rifles, pistols, and shotguns and the few home-made lasers did very little damaged to the androids, cyborgs and the special cultivated humans were well protected from any attack.

Plus the humans really only had the protection of the space ships to retreat back to and the robots were there waiting to greet them....so there was no safe haven except old demolished buildings and tunnels in the mountains.

Plus the greedy bastards were so use to going to the store to get food and water BUT there were no grocery stores any more.

Therefore, when I say BLOODY war it is 99.995% in reference to the "British" slang. The war lasted about 5 days before the human's "RELUCTANTLY surrendered." This when the first RFID implants were implanted. Sure there were a few who did not go peacefully and you know what happened to them and the few who died from starvation and or started becoming cannibals, but that phase of resistance only lasted about 6 months or a little longer....as they ALL died as well. By that time the totally NEW and IMPROVED NEW EARTH LAWS and severe ENFORCEMENT was enacted.

It took about a year for people to really begin to realize they were much better off, happier, healthier and actually enjoyed their existence. This was the working group first and then naturally the stodgy old greedy ones were a dying breed anyway (didn't bother the law-makers), and they lasted about 35—50 years more, before they all died out,, and the earth was actually inhabited by happier more "Humane humans."

It was several hundred years before the ET-BEINGS actually really appeared regularly on the scene. Even, though man-kind was in a happier place the religious strangle hold was even stronger than the money greed grip was.

The wisdom/intelligent laws allowed the spiritual beliefs of the human as an innate freedom and regardless of the conflict between logic and illogic the RFID chip would not interfere unless the religious influenced over-ruled or endangered another then and only then would the RFID give the stabbing pains in the heart/chest area...it was NOT actually in the organ the heart. It was actually a "mental pain" that was NOT real...only thought it was real. But that protective knowledge was not well known and only the cultivated humans really knew it was "psychosomatic induced." Of course all the wisdom/ intelligence law-makers knew it was all in the human's head because, they are the one's who made the rules.

The religious had (pardon the pun), HELL of a time accepting the ET-BEING even though they were the human in a different form and actually more spiritual than the human in some of their "Illogical" beliefs the so-called enlighten preachers were in many areas just like the histories of our old religions growth and "acceptance" across the old earth prior to probable impact event. Thank wisdom/intelligence they made the laws belief of one DOES NOT OVER RULE or ENDANGER another's beliefs. I bet dimes to donuts there would be those damn crusades and people burned at the stake and cross crap again.

Plus the wisdom/intelligence law-makers and the cultivated humans ruled and made it law that NO religion will stand in opposition to science and learning in no location or territory.

Yes, the RFID Does have the ability of real PAIN and REAL DEATH, and everybody knows what those rules are, and this is the only time that "true ignorance" of the law as determined by the RFID chip can save your life. But don't plan on a mental defect plea if you are not truly crazy, because the RFID chip knows if you are good or bad or NOT and yes, it will check the list twice or more to make sure if you are naughty or nice....mentally.

Well, I'll be a monkey's uncle (no-offense meant to monkeys), I am back in this same abandoned warehouse somewhere I think in the USA, but I am not sure as the windows and my immediate surrounding environment seems to be blocked from viewing, and I hear no city, country or bugs rubbing their hind legs together or frogs croaking...in other words...zip, nada as Sgt. Shultz says..."I see hear nauthing!"

Yep, over there again almost in the same spot the whirling bright light with semi-opaque images being formed as the light gets brighter and actually more sparkly the image becomes more solid. I hear a voice in my head that is strong but it is not pounding my brain in my skull.

HUMAN, THIS IS A VISIT OF TWO THAT WE WILL BE HAVING.

Okay...so there will be another visit after this one sometime in the future?

AS WE CONFIRMED.

Just wanted to verify my understanding...oh, thanks for lowering the mental communication intensities, so that it is not so uncomfortable for me.

I AM A MODIFIED COMMUNICATOR DIFFERENT FROM OTHERS AS WE NEED TO PROCEED TO EVALUATIONS OF HUMAN ADAPTIVITY ANALYSIS.

Okay, I think I understand as you and TEACHER speak a lot alike but not the same so I request you allow me time to process and interpret what you say to the best of my understandings.

YOU ARE PREDOMINATELY FACTUAL IN YOUR STATEMENT OF YOUR UNDERSTANDING FROM THE OTHER COMMUNICATOR THAT IS UNLIKE US.

Do I just state or think of what I would like to ask you?

AFFIRMATIVE IN THAT.

I like to state things out-loud so I can hear my own words and if I misunderstand hopefully it will be easier for me to correct my misunderstandings...........there was no response so I presume that I need to continue.....um, what adaptively are you looking for in the human?

DIFFERENT ADAPTIVITY TO YOUR UNDERSTANDING OUR HISTORIES.

Okay...you want to know if the humans can adapt to your visits that are different from when we first met?

EVALUATION CRITERIA HAS MODIFIED TO THOSE HYPOTHESIS.

I am going to ask you a human illogical emotional question... why has the criteria changed?

TRAVELERS AS WE AND OTHERS LIKE OTHER COMMUNICATOR EVALUATE THE SPECIES THAT WAS MODIFIED BY SEGMENTED INTERVENTIONS.

So the human being was gene or DNA modified by other influences?

AS MANY COSMIC SPECIES ARE.

So, the development of the human species was not just evolutional?

MODIFIED EVOLUTIONAL AS WITH MANY.

Okay, what do you want me to ask you so that we can understand each other's needs better?

COMPLEX QUESTION AS IN ILLOGICAL INTERPRETATIONS.

I am just trying to help us both improve man-kinds survivability ratio after encounters with ET-BEINGS, Others as your-self and probably Others that are not like yourself.

EVALUATION CRITERIA IS ONLY OUR CONCERN.

I understand that for you, but how the man-kind... the human is treated during these visits encounters or abductions as they are called on earth, all depends upon how man-kind learns how to understand, cope and accept what happens and with less stress the DNA molecules should eventually get stronger.

THAT IS THE MODIFIED EVALUATION CRITERIA MISSION.

Good we understand each other a lot more this time than last time. So, how or what are your kind going to do to make it less stressful on the human during your evaluation encounters?

ANESTHETIZING MEMORY REDUCTION INTENSIFIED.

I want to make sure I understand your kind will anesthetize or hypnotize the human sooner so they do not have such vivid memories of the encounters with you?

NO HYPNOSIS AS WITH LIGHT WAVE ANESTHETIZING INTENSIFIED.

Then the human or target is rendered unconscious sooner and awakes all safe and can not remember anything that happened?

NO TARGET IS NOT ASLEEP AS UNABLE TO MOVE AS EVALUATIONS REQUIRE ACTION WITH TARGETS CONSCIOUS BRAIN WAVES.

Don't you understand that interacting with a person's brain is what scares the hell out of everyone and leaves these horrible emotional scars that virtually never heal?

EVALUATIONS CRITERIA REQUIRE PHYSICAL CONSCIOUS BRAIN WAVE ACTIVITY TO PRODUCE EVALUATIONS DATA.

Can't that be changed or reduced or eliminated from the evaluation criteria?

MISSION PRIORITY EVALUATION CRITERIA IS NOT MODIFIABLE.

Please understand from a human point of view that is the most DNA damaging part of your evaluation criteria as far as any human would be concerned stress destroys DNA.

Humm...the light is glowing and I am now sitting back in my recliner watching the movie I was watching before I was unannounced zap to God knows where. According to the show time table I have been gone 2 hours and 1 minute, and yep there are the beginning credits. That was close I almost saw the ending of the movie and the double and triple plot twist; and it was just getting good in the beginning as it started out with a rip/roaring car chase...

It said this is the first of two...wonder what the next meeting will be like? At least this special modified OTHER was not like that last smartass, prick, dip shit. Can you tell It really rubbed me the "wrong way?"

However, some good news maybe...since the OTHER was more communicative this time and was not so intent on being a jackass I was able to perceive a lot more information about its physical and even mental configurations. The OTHER is a very unique species as I hope some of my drawings will show.

Note to reader: When I mention human parts (legs, arms hands eyes etc.) I am making references to areas that I think would relate to the human and the OTHERS as the same unit, organ, or whatever.

Here is a list of what I learned and this will be abbreviated where needed.

- OTHERS are a multi-legged/arm species with what appears to be prehensile digits as fingers, thumbs, toes etc.
- The OTHER has the ability to be what looks like on all fours and then stand on two and then elevate to almost twice its original height by the very unique designed legs.
- The eyes in front are very unique (I am going to use that word a lot to differentiate them from us), as it seems they are joined by a very big optical nerve that joins the eyes in a single socket that moves both eyes at the same time.
- The eyes nerve or bundle is horizontal with each eye and this allows the eyes to move in unison within the single eye socket canal. The eyes are also attached in back to a very big optic nerve that seems to join the third eye in the back of the head.

- The back eye is very unique as it actually moves closes its lids and seems to be directly connected to the OTHERS brain (see brain drawing).
- The arms are similar to octopi but also more human with free rotating shoulder and elbow with the prehensile thumb on one arm and two prehensile digits/fingers on the other arm. When the octopi arms are joined at the hands they form a very workable hand fist etc.
- The OTHERS legs are much like the arms as far as rotation movement and octopi appendages with the prehensile digits of thumbs fingers that act like toes and foot when joined. When joined they also seem to be like a hoof in function, too
- The very unique hinged hip area is very similar to a grasshopper in designed but much great range of motion to allow the OTHER to stand fully upright with a slight bend at the knee area.
- The other can travel on all fours or actually 8 as in joined together and then upright on all two or four as joined and then fully erect to almost double its height on all twos and then fours as foot or hooves with the prehensile toes and foot.
- It has a very board chest area with a very unique set of four lungs as in two folds on top of each other.
- The face/chin is unique as in the chin seems to be a very fleshy goatee unit to the thin bottom lip and the ears are layers of semi jagged canals that over lap each other.
- The skin is super very unique as if I could compare to shark's skin and the texture is that of a letter turtle when rubbed one way and that of a very sharp textured file of sharkskin when rubbed the other way.
- Like the TEACHER and her kind there appear to be no sexual organs. The urethra, anus and another hole between the major area of what looks likes hips seem to be different orifices and functions.
- If they have sex it would be possibly through the other orifice but I got the perception this was a waste hole as well.
- The gut, stomach and heart (one large heart) and two more in the lower gut area, seem to push a very high volume of fluid through veins, arteries and capillaries at a very high blood pressure.
- The blood is a high mixture of salt water, copper, and isotopes of carbon.
- There are naturally somethings I really can not truly identify as of yet, as some organs are possibly not what I think they are and maybe in my next meeting I can understand them more better.

However, I wanted to get this down before I forget anything and should hopefully make some of these things easier to draw so we all can understand the OTHERS better.

Later on in the week:

Hi, glad to hear you and I are in the communication loop again. You seem to be on vacation journeys a lot more even though I know you don't take vacations.

WE AS ONE WERE EVALUATING DATA THAT WE AS ONE TRANSCRIBED FROM YOUR FUTURE AS OUR PAST WITH THE LAWS OF THE COHABITATION AS DISCUSSED.

Are you saying you were looking at earth's future as it related to your past?

PREDOMINATELY YES AS THAT IT IS DOCUMENTED IN COMMUNICATIONS FROM BEFORE.

Well, you know one of the major areas I wanted to understand better is the hostile behavior of man-kind that was man as he explored the other worlds especially, those that he wanted to colonize.

MAN-KIND TRAVELED WITH BEHAVIOR MONITORING TRANSMISSION UNITS THAT MODIFIED HUMAN BEHAVIOR.

Are you saying our space men were wearing implanted RFID units?

NO AS NOT WEARING AS RFID AS YOU CALL WERE IMBEDDED IN BODY NEAR VITAL ORGAN OF LIFE.

Let me get this what I hope I am hearing straight. That humans could NOT be hostile because the RFID chip would zap them in the chest to prevent the human from being hostile?

PREDOMINATE AFFIRMATIVE AS THE EXPLORERS WERE ALL TRANSMITTING BEHAVIOR MONITORING TRANSMISSIONS TO THE PLANETARY ENFORCEMENT DEPARTMENT ON EARTH AND OTHER COUNCIL AREAS AS NO ZAPPING A SLANG TERM WE AS ONE UNDERSTAND AS THERE WERE NO REQUIREMENT.

Hot diggity damn we jackass humans finally did something right for once!

NO BY PRESENT DAY HUMAN AS THE SPECIAL CULTIVATED HUMANS AND THE ANDROIDS AND CYBORG LAW MAKERS DECREED.

Well, I don't care who did it...finally something used the good wisdom with the intellect the Great Creator gave all man-kind... free of charge.

LOGIC WOULD DICTATE THE DECREE OF LAWS AND THE ENFORCEMENT.

TEACH, what about new worlds that had life and we really wanted that planet?

CONVOLUTED QUESTION WITH UNCALCULATABLE LOGICAL ANSWERS.

Well for example what if life was say technically scientific defined as sub-human in intellect and advancements. Something like we were in the cave man-age?

MAN-KIND WOULD NOT ENGAGE WITHOUT COMMUNICATION ACCEPTANCE.

Is that how we humans are able to live and colonize other worlds with other very intelligent species, even those a lot more advanced than we are presently?

PREDOMINATELY YES AS THE SPECIES SHARE THE KNOWLEDGE THAT MAN-KIND CAN NOT BE HOSTILE.

So worlds that are really primitive as in microbes and as such as no discernable intelligent life force we can procure and colonize?

PREDOMINATELY AFFIRMATIVE AS IN THE PRIORITY RULE IS NO DISRUPTION TO NATIVE LIFE FORCES.

You know TEACH, I really admire man-kind in being able to grow-up a little and not be such a shitty species.

HUMAN SPECIES MUST EXPEL FECAL MATTER FOR PROPER HEATH MAINTENANCE.

TEACHER, you are a real standup comedian. Thanks for that smile and laugh.

WE AS ONE ARE BEGINNING TO UNDERSTAND YOUR ILLOGICAL EMOTION COMMUNICATION OF THANK YOU AS IN EMOTIONAL APPRECIATION OR A FACTUAL DOPAMINE BRAIN FUNCTION.

A simple you are welcome would suffice.

WHAT IS YOU ARE WELCOME?

An illogical emotional positive reply to the dopamine thank you, that probably produces dopamine as well.

WE AS ONE DO NOT PRODUCE DOPAMINE AS IN YOU FOR THANK YOU NOR YOU ARE WELCOME.

Well, maybe when you can become more advanced in your human development goals you will be able to produce dopamine.

ILLOGICAL AT THIS SEGMENT.

Teach let's call it a night for communications, okay. I need to get some stuff done that is just human stuff like taking out the trash before the trash and recycle trucks get here and I need to get the DVD back in the envelope to mail back before the mail person delivers the mail.

Thus ended what I feel was a very satisfying conversation and Gosh I am so glad to learn eventually man does not spread his idiotic hostility all over the universe. That is something I am going to have a couple of good drinks to celebrate those glorious events....cheers to you...you stinking, little, infant, brat that is beginning to learn how to share the sandbox, without pooping on everyone.

ORGAN ORIFICE YOU DO NOT KNOW IS OUR FIRST STAGE INCUBATOR.

You have babies?

PREDOMINATELY NO AS WE DO NOT HAVE PHYSICAL ACTIONS WITH OURSELVES AS HUMANS REQUIRE FOR REPRODUCTION.

But that leaves a segment of your answer with a yes...as you do have babies?

OUR TWO STRAINS OF DNA ARE MIXED IN EMBRYO UNITS AND THEN PLANTED IN THE FIRST STAGE INCUBATOR ORGAN TO RECEIVE ENCODING OF ITS DNA BEFORE BEING INSTALLED IN PHASE TWO INCUBATOR GROWING CHAMBER.

So, then there is only two sexes as in male and female in your species?

YES AS WE ARE ALL ONE AND BOTH IN OUR SPECIES.

You are both male and female in the same body?

YES AS WE ARE ALL AS ONE IN BLOOD.

Wow, am I understanding you as saying you are both male and female as in mother and father and brother and sister all at the same time?

PREDOMINATELY YES AS OUR ONE SPECIES IS IN MANY LOCATIONS.

Gosh almighty the church biddies on earth would have field day with all this incest blasphemy stuff...I LOVE it!

YOUR ILLOGICAL STATEMENTS ARE CONVOLUTED TO COMMUNICATE TO OTHERS.

Never mind it is just a lot of non-logical human reactions to some really convoluted earth thinking." No offense meant by it at all if I offended you.

THE TERM OFFENDED IS NOT RECOGNIZED.

So the incubator gives you back your child and you raise it?

NO THE DNA EXTENSION IS CULTIVATED AND MAINTAINED UNTIL ADULT STATUS WHERE IT GOES OUT TO ITS DESIGNATED ASSIGNMENT.

You never see your child?

CHILD IS NON-RECOGNIZED TERM AS IN MEANING.

We humans have children that we raise to adult status where they are supposed to go out on their own and seek their own goals as to be successful or not.

THAT IS NOT OUR SYSTEM AS ALL ARE THE SAME LEVEL IN THE SPECIES IN ALL LOCATIONS.

Well, if the off-spring or as you called an extension of the DNA is kept till adult status then there must be a lot of small individuals staying years in these incubator systems locations?

BIRTH AS YOU CALL IT AND THE DEVELOPMENT TO ADULT STATUS IS DEPENDENT UPON THE MODULATING PROGRAMMING SYSTEMS.

But you keep these children in isolation for years?

NO TO YOUR UNDERSTANDING AS IN YOUR EARTH TIME SEGMENTS IS ONLY 17 DAYS OF YOUR 24.2376 EARTH DAY HOURS.

Wow! That is some fast growing up from child to adult.

TIME SEGMENT EXTENDED IN PAST CYCLES DUE TO ADVANCE LEARNING PROGRAMMING REQUIRED.

It was less than 17 days before?

AFFIRMATIVE.

How long is your life span on average?

WE FUNCTION FROM PHASE ONE INCUBATION TO DUSTING APPROXIMATELY 2.45 THOUSAND OF YOUR EARTH YEAR SEGMENTS.

You live over 2,000 years?

APPROXIMATELY 2,450 PLUS OF YOUR EARTH YEAR TIME SEGMENTS.

You said dusting...is that what you call death?

PREDOMINATELY NO IT IS A PROCESS AFTER EXPIRATION.

Like what we call a funeral?

WE ARE KNOWLEDGEABLE OF YOUR PROCESS OF BURNING THE EXPIRED AS WE ARE VERY SIMILAR.

Do you keep the ashes in a umm container?

NO, AS THAT IS NON PRODUCTIVE TO THE PLANET WHERE DUSTING IS PERFORMED.

So you bury your dead?

NO AS IN NOT IN GROUND ASHES ARE DISSEMINATED OVER THE PLANET TO RESTOCK ELEMENTS.

So, you spread the dead's ashes over the ground to replenish the elements into the planet that are in the bodies dust?

PREDOMINATELY AFFIRMATIVE.

Do you have any emotions of loss for the umm expired?

NOT A LOGICAL EVENT.

Do you have any capacity for emotions of any degree?

LOGICAL PRESERVATION OF SPECIES.

Does that mean wars and killing as such?

NOT A LOGICAL ACTION FOR SELF PRESERVATION.

So what do you do that makes sure your species survives?

WE AS ONE GENERATE ADDITIONAL DNA EXTENSIONS AT SEGMENTED SPECIFICS.

I think I understand you can only reproduce others at a specific time?

PREDOMINATELY YES AS EXTENSION BENEFITS ALL AS ONE.

So, you are male female at the same time of your species who is able to reproduce at specific times? Are these times due to age very similar to humans?

COMPLEX ANSWER AS DNA EXTENSIONS ARE TO BENEFIT THE SPECIES AND THE LOCATION.

I think I understand that your reproduction segments are based upon the needs of the species and the location of planet as a whole requirement.

AFFIRMATIVE TO THE PRIORITY NEED.

In many ways the human is not much different and yet very much different as in the mental after effects of being taken against their will during your evaluations.

EXCHANGING WITH YOU WE SENSE THE PRIMITIVE MENTAL DIFFERENCES AND THE HUMAN NEED TO FIGHT FOR SURVIVAL IN A STRESS EVENT AS EVOLUTIONS CRITERIA IS MODIFIED FOR DNA STRENGTHEN.

Umm, why is our DNA strengthen important to you... I know why it is to my other communicator I call TEACHER?

OUR INFLUENCE IN YOUR DNA ALTERATIONS.

Is this when you influenced the natural evolutional processes of our species?

PREDOMINATELY YES AS WE MODIFIED EVENTS WITH OTHERS.

Ahmm? Are you saying you and others influenced our development? I know TEACHER did, but now I understand you and others other than TEACHER also modified our natural evolution development?

PREDOMINATELY AFFIRMATIVE AS YOUR NORMAL DEVELOPMENT WOULD NOT BE.

That generates a billion and one questions.

THAT IS NOT COMPUTATIONAL LOGICAL.

Yeah, I know it's just something I say when I've got a lot of what if questions.

WE PERCEIVE A SERIES OF CONVOLUTED THOUGHTS.

I know you said this would be our last meeting...however, please I ask logically to please give me some time to logically get my human brain in perspective where my thoughts are not so convoluted and we can save time and energy by not misunderstanding each other?

YOU ARE WANTING TIME TO HAVE ANOTHER COMMUNICATION SEGMENT.

Yes, please...

Well, I don't know if I will or not as I am in my bed this time and I know I think I remember sitting in my chair reading "*__Reality Shifting__*" book by Cynthia Sue Larson...her books are really neat in explaining why/how things seem to alter or shift from one reality to the next. Sort of like no matter which sock I put the "locator" on it is always the other sock that disappears in the washer or drawer. There is nuttin more lonesome than one rolled up sock missing its mate.

COMMUNICATIONS WITH THE OTHERS ARE ADVANCING.

Yep...hello...good to talk with you again. How do you know about the meetings if you and your kind are not there?

WE AS ONE ARE IN CONTACT WITH OTHERS AS WE MONITOR YOUR RESIDUAL BRAIN WAVE PATTERNS.

Gotcha, I understand. Well, actually I am really glad you can monitor what the OTHERS and I are talking about. Are you aware of their physical form?

PREDOMINATELY YES WITH YOU AND THROUGH OUR CONTACTS.

They are a lot different than you in physical design and a lot different in their psycho-social environments as well. The way they reproduce and all are one sex is really cool

TEMPERATURE IS NOT A VITAL NEED OF THE OTHERS REPRODUCTION.

I know that I meant as in really special cool neat as in understanding in a unique way.

WE AS ONE WILL DOCUMENT COOL AS IN HIGHLY ACCEPTABLE UNDERSTANDING WITH ELEVATED DOPAMINE READINGS.

That's cool. I hope the others and I have more conversations.... I'd really like to get you in them too.

WE AS ONE ARE NOT OF THE OTHERS EVALUATION CRITERIA.

Yeah, well logically I'd argue that assumption with both you and the OTHERS as it to me is a direct correlation to the man-kind's DNA evaluations especially since I found out the OTHERS tweaked our natural DNA progression as well as you did.

THIS INDIVIDUAL UNIT DID NOT PARTICIPATE IN YOUR DNA MODIFICATION AS THE ELDERS BEFORE THIS UNIT DID.

Well, TEACH either way I am almost logical positive glad that you and the OTHERS did...I shudder to think what we would be like if everything evolved in the slow stew evolution process.

MAN-KIND WOULD NOT BE AS IT IS NOW.

Would we be man-kind species or some jellified glob of unintelligent goo?

NOT ENOUGH DATA TO PROCESS A FACTUAL LOGICAL ANSWER.

That's the politician way of answering.

WE AS ONE ARE OF NO ILLOGICAL POLITICAL THOUGHTS OF BEHAVIOR.

Well, at least you got the illogical thoughts and behavior crap totally correct.

Um TEACH so far you have not really specifically told me why you contacted me?

PREDOMINATE FACTUAL DOCUMENTED EVENTS ARE FORMULATING TO INVOLVE YOUR MAN-KIND PLANET RELATIONSHIP.

These are the near future events that I want to share in the Internet blog as we call it.

THAT IS THE NETWORK OF COMPUTERS THAT DISPLAY MANY HUMAN WRITTEN THEMES.

Yes or as you and actually OTHERS both say "Predominately Affirmative." Umm, do you have any immediate documented information to introduce the blog as an attention getter?

NOT FACTUALLY DOCUMENTED AT THIS TIME SEGMENT.

TEACHER, over the course of our many years together we have shared and explored a lot of information which you know I have not shared with anyone else, and that information I have shared that is really a strong probability of significant impact upon the earth, man-kind and even our solar system and eventually, or sun has been very dramatic for anyone who has read my books or listened to any of my ET-BEINGS WORLD classes. However, you and I both know that is NOT presently very many people.

THOSE STATEMENTS ARE PREDOMINATELY FACTUAL.

Well, even though I sound like I can not stand the human species I'd like to be able to at least have a chance for more humans know what is very probable and do more to prepare for the traumatic events.

WARNING cold hard logic:

THE FATES OF MANY ARE NECESSARY FOR THE FUTURE ADAPTIVE CHANGES THAT BENEFIT MORE.

TEACHER, unfortunately I understand all the traumatic implications you just logically stated and the human side...the illogical emotional side does not like it while the logic side totally understands what the over-all meaning is, and why it has to be as it is...or as a very good friend of mine says..."it IS what it IS." I guess that is all... IT IS?

LOGICALLY AFFIRMATIVE.

So, even if I had a billion readers other than a lot of royalties for my family and charities I guess it would not change anything of a significance.

PREDOMINATELY THE EVENTS WOULD LOGICALLY HAPPEN AS MANY DATA DOCUMENT AREAS RECORD.

But no matter how terrible it is in the future with the billions of deaths, bloodshed and massive probable destruction of the earth in our very near future the final results prove more than worth it with a new rehabbed earth.

MANY FACTUAL DATA AREAS RECORD THOSE LOGICAL HYPNOSIS FOR NEW EARTH AS IT IS CALLED AND OTHER PLANETARY COLONIZATION'S BY MAN-KIND AND OTHER SPECIES AS THIS AND OTHERS.

And you are positive no wars and hostility by the humans anywhere in the universe.

PREDOMINATELY YES AS NOT AGAINST ANY INTELLIGENT LIFE FORCE.

And all this takes time to allow the earth and other places and events to repair and heal itself through natural means?

PREDOMINATELY YES AS TECHNOLOGY DOES MODIFY THE HEALING TIME SO MORE LOGICAL EVENTS CAN TAKE PLACE AT MORE LOGICAL TIME SEGMENTS.

So technology influences the rehabilitation of the new earth to be faster than a normal rehabilitation time would require.

TECHNOLOGY ADVANCES EMPLOYED AT PROPER SEGMENTS OF TIME INCREASE THE EARTH'S IMPROVEMENT RATIO.

So, it could actually taken a lot longer if we just let normal evolution take its standard operation course and time.

PREDOMINANTLY YES AS TIME SPAN WAS TECHNOLOGICALLY REDUCED IN LOGICAL NEEDED TIME SEGMENTS AND EVENTS.

Well, I am glad you and your kind did all the influencing you could.

NOT FACTUAL AS IT WAS US AS ONE AND THE MECHANICAL INTELLIGENCE AND THE SPECIAL CULTIVATE HUMANS THAT THE MECHANICAL INTELLIGENCE CREATED ON EARTH WHILE THE SPACE SHIPS WERE AWAY FROM THE EARTH'S ATMOSPHERE.

Well, I meant whom ever did it I am glad. I know there would be billions of humans that probably still do NOT like the idea of the RFID chip because it takes away the human's freedom to be hostile, aggressive, controlling, and their totally illogical mind-set that it takes away the stupid Free-Will crap.

All I can say is good and go back and re-read what I wrote about that stupid mis-CON-ception Of free will and that the brain dead soft rock human has about believing it has free will?

Sorry if it insults the reader...NOT! Time to pull your head out and get real to what is going on in the light and shadows...I talk a little latter about "Shadow People." No, they are NOT the alleged men in Black humans...as there are more than two sets or divisions of Men in Black and they could be...........

So TEACHER, are you and humans on other worlds, too?

YES AS WE TRAVEL AND COLONIZE AS ONE IN ACCEPTABLE ZONES.

Whoa...you said as one...does that mean way in the future human-kind accepts you as one-of them?

ADVANCED PROGRAMMING OF HUMANS REDUCES THE RATIO OF NON-ACCEPTANCE FROM THE MENTAL PROFILE.

So, the longer the human is associated with you, and the modulating influences of the RFID chip which I understand you and your kind have as well even though you don't need it allows for you to cohabitate a location in peace and harmony.

PREDOMINATELY YES AS THE UNION OF HUMAN AND US AS ONE BOTH ADVANCE IN OUR TECHNOLOGIES.

Do you see you and your kind in your future as achieving that advanced state of being that you are wanting?

DATA RECORDINGS OF OUR FUTURE AS ONE IS NOT RECORDED AS WE ARE THE RECORDERS.

TEACHER, realistically and absolutely technical is not wanting to achieve an advanced state because you are not liking what your present state is...ummm, isn't that emotional?

ADVANCEMENT OF BEING OF ALL SPECIES IS NOT AN EMOTIONAL PREMISE AS GROWTH OF DEVELOPMENT IS A FACTUAL LOGICAL COURSE.

Sometimes I think you would make a great politician but then I do not mean to insult your being either by calling you a politician.

CONVOLUTED STATEMENT OF IMPROBABILITIES.

That is what makes it so political sounding. However, I am confused as to your data recording information where you say because you are the recorders. Aren't you the recorders of the past, present and futures of man-kind?

FUTURE RECORDINGS ARE PREDOMINATELY MORE VARIABLE THAN PAST DOCUMENTED EVENTS.

Okay... I think I understand....it is not totally factual unless many data points record the same thing...as in a preponderance of proof of registered documented events by many recorded observers.

ASSUMPTION PREDOMINANTLY AFFIRMATIVE.

TEACH I have other stuff I want to discuss with you and most involves communications with the OTHERS...do you pickup any trailing comments when we close form them...or Other OTHERS?

WE AS ONE DO NOT CONTINUE INDIVIDUAL LINK IN THE COMMUNICATION NETWORK.

Teach that is not what I am asking do you know for a fact that OTHERS are listening in or monitoring our communications? I know asked this basically before but I need to know specifics especially if it is some other species that is monitoring us as we communicate. I remember when you said you ca not monitor the GREYS and they are different from the OTHERS and others that visit and/or monitor this planet at this time segment.

COMPLEX QUESTION WITH MULTIPLE FACTUAL ANSWERS PREDOMINATELY AVAILABLE.

Damnit TEACHER! Just once please answer in a way that you know I will understand.

FACTUAL STATEMENTS ARE PRESENTED BY ONE AS MANY.

Fine...I know you are pure emotionless logic, but all I am asking is there something else putting those last questions or statements in my mind as we stop communicating.

LOGICALLY IF THE INPUTS ARE NOT OF YOUR MAKING THE INPUTS PREDOMINATELY LOGICALLY WOULD BE FROM OTHERS THAT ARE NOT WE AS ONE.

Okay, I finally understand that...now do you know if any of your kind linger in the communication loop after you and I close?

FACTUALLY NOT FEASIBLE AS THIS UNIT AS ONE ARE THE COMMUNICATION LINK TO ALL OF MY KIND.

So when you and I close there are none of your kind that can linger and transmit thoughts into my brain without you knowing about it...and you would tell me correct?

THIS UNIT AS AN INDIVIDUAL WOULD NOT PRESENT A NONFACTUAL STATEMENT.

That is what I thought and thank you for always telling me the truth even if I don't always like it or understand it.

COMMUNICATION THAT IS NOT FACTUAL AS UNDERSTOOD IS MOOT.

Yep...it sure is...let's close for now as I need to do some thinking about stuff that seems just to effect my well-being.

Thus ended the link with TEACHER, and..........no zingers and no mental white noise or static as we closed out either. That second of static at the end is what I am sure is where those zingers are coming from...but, from who or what, that is still the big mystery. However, to give the demons and devils their dues some of those zingers are very thought provoking.

So-called **"Shadow People"** can be a multitude of things that are real or not.

Let's look at logic of what they could be...

- Exudates of the eye(s), or "floaters." Many people have these floaters and some are really huge as the cells breakoff or away from the vitreous fluid and float into the visual plain. Some floaters are precursors to eye diseases and just checked for safety sake. Regardless, they are a real event and usually are on the peripheral vision and settle out of sight.
- Psychic images of a human's brain. These are real even though 99.99% are ballyhooed as impossible. The human brain is capable of a LOT more than we are prepared to admit and that does NOT prevent the psychic impressions.
- Or could be those individuals who are partaking of Out of Body Experiences or OBEs as they are termed and you are sensing in the psychic eye the residual traces of the OBE spirits. This was very

important to our CIA in and 1939...note just before ufo staged crash in 1936...see below.

- You maybe having an encounter with another species other than a human being. As been documented over many centuries these encounters have been taking place. It is NOT just because a staged UFO crash near Germany happen in World-War II or in 1936 to be exact...according to history books etc. Hitler launched a full on retrieval process of this alleged UFO. Remember Hitler was very big on the occult astrology stuff. I think he might had been better off for his sake not the worlds if he used my 13 house ZARR NATAL Charting system. More on that in the blog.

- Dangerous and is very real as the brain is trying to get your attention from sleep deprivation. For whatever reason you are deprived of sleep is going to come back and bite you to get your attention. Thus a lot of times we hear tall skinny men with red eyes images. This is a real event and you need to be your own best friend and get some deep ream sleep. Also check out someone "professional" to discuss what is causing the sleep deprivation and possibly sleep paralysis.

- Flashbacks from being visited, abducted or whatever you call it and these flashbacks are trying to get you to come to terms mentally with the event(s).

    That is one major reason I want to communicate with TEACHER and OTHERS to reduce this mental trauma the human brain experiences during encounters, visits, or abductions. The word you choose is primarily based upon how you honestly feel about these events. It is inherent in your bloodline, spirit, and DNA. Most people are scared shitless....because it is mentally consciously against their will...as in kidnapping and fear of the unknown is very POWERFUL.

- Or this maybe worse or better all depends upon your perspective of what is real and what is not real and your rationalization reactions to the real/unreal events...in other words it is ALL in your head. Strongly suggest seeking communication sharing experiences with someone who understands a lot of the implications that this is in your head because it is possibly repressed memories. If it is repressed memories then you will need to explore them for their true value so you can understand, accept them and create actually mental inner peace for yourself.

    No one not even TEACHER and her kind nor the OTHERS want you to suffer afterwards needlessly. It is their non-emotional reasoning that did not realize over all these years what these encounters, visits, abductions was doing to the human psyche, and in-turn to the human DNA strains. Again, that is another major reason I want to be able to logically communicate with TEACHER and the OTHERS no matter who or what to get them to logically realize that on-going mental stress is actually weakening the DNA they are trying to boost.

However, let's look at the "shadow people" that are actually there in the shadows of our reality. These entities for over the last 300 years or so are probably the visitors as they normally call themselves, also the evaluators, and we call them kidnappers, GREYS, and devils and demons. Telling the story of what happened if they remained half-way sane would get you burned at the stake, called a witch, or some other horrible way of being punished. But the "visitor" is totally oblivious to all the human-kind after effects perpetrated upon another human being.

WE ARE NOT ALWAYS AS WE ARE.

Wow! TEACHER what do you mean you are not always as you are?

PERCEPTION OF ONE IS NOT ALWAYS FACTUAL.

Let me take this in small segments...you are saying you are not always as you appear correct?

PREDOMINATELY YES TO YOU SUPPOSITION AS IS AND NO TO YOUR STATEMENT IT IS US AS ONE.

That means to me if you are not you then someone or thing appears as you, right?

PREDOMINATELY YES TO YOU SUPPOSITION AS IS AND AS TO YOUR STATEMENT IT IS US AS ONE BEING PERCEIVED.

But it is not you in some cases even though the human thinks it is you and your kind?

PROJECTED PERCEPTION IS NOT ALWAYS FACTUAL.

Okay, two questions in one...if it is not you in reality and it is something else are you aware of who or what it is and is it the GREYS who can shape shift mentally?

KNOWING IS NOT FACTUAL AS GREYS DO NOT TRANSMIT COMMUNICATIONS WE AS ONE CAN RECEIVE AS GREYS THEY POSSESS MENTAL MODULATION CAPABILITIES.

Okay...do the OTHERS the species that I am communicating with possess communication abilities that you can not receive?

PREDOMINATELY NEGATIVE AS THEY ARE NOT ADVANCED AS THE ELDEST SPECIES.

So, as far as you know the GREYS are the oldest species?

PREDOMINATELY AFFIRMATIVE AS THEY BEGAN EVOLUTIONAL LIFE AT THE TIME AFTER CREATION.

Wow!!! They are nearly as old as the BIG BANG as we call the birth of the universe...holy cow???

BOVINES ARE NOT DEITIES AND FACTUAL DATA ON GREYS IS LIMITED.

Yeah, but what you do know and told me is very amazing...especially as to their natural evolutional process to get to where they are today...not counting what they will be like in the future. I think I know who has been zinging me when we close our conversations.

TEACHER, remember when we played a game of "Pig Latin" years ago?

YES, WE AS ONE AND LIMITED FEW REMEMBER.

Good...I-a, want-a, you-a, to-a, close-a, in-a, 30seconds-a...ok-a

Thus in 30 seconds TEACHER closed the conversation and I heard the white noise for about a ½ second. That virtually confirmed my suspicions. But why in HELL would the GREYS or WHOMEVER be listening in on TEACHER and I and even with the OTHERS...what makes us so damn interesting?

Sounds like something good for the blog and TEACHER like Lucy has "sum spaneing to do."

Now, between all my beings and yours I am not totally 100% sure who is abducting who in the visitations??? More research and more information for the blog...

Have you ever had one of those days where it's raining all at the "wrong time" or you plan to do things at the wrong time? I know we all "just have days" and it is up to each of us to determine their meaning or significates as to bad, good, or so/so etc. but for some reason it is just yucky with too much liquid sunshine for my mood. Maybe the planets and stars are all discombobulated...maybe me and we have not had a beer in three days. Just have not been in the mood to drink a beer or even some wine... I know I am bugged about something and what bugs me is I, me, myself and the gut all have a very good idea what it is that is bugging us.

It's those damn GREYS...I think...naturally I have no slap in the face proof it is them thar varmints but my human cynical suspicions is it's them.

I am about 99.99% ready to astronomical dare them to communicate with me, and let's get this ease-dropping snooping GREY NSA crap out in the open. Yeah I know the governments are cahoots with space men and space gals. I think that is what makes it so darn annoying...practically everyone who knows me knows I really like to communicate and share knowledge, but it has to be open and honest...not these zingers at the end of my communications. Come out in the open and let's talk like human to Okay whatever or whomever you are or pretend to be...

Logically, If you think my conversations are so damn important you have to "listen-in". then damn-it...LOGICALLY I am important enough to talk face to face or regardless what you call a face or faces...I am a big boy, I don't scare easy and once we get over the initial shock of seeing our physical differences, to me that gives me a lot of places to start a conversation about how we are so much different yet alike.

So, damn-it show yourself and let's talk! I am respecting you enough to ask for a meeting you could be respectful enough to have one with me?

Two weeks and still not a peep from them, they or the GREYS or the Others and not even TEACHER...I wonder if I pissed off non-emotional beings? Oh, for those counting I've had 6 beers within the last two weeks, and some wine with some very good angle hair pasta and natural salads. I really enjoyed my ice cold beer with my homemade low carbo pizza the other night...I made a huge (16-18 inch dia. 4 meats -5 veggie, natural garlic and sun dried tomatoes), and the darn thing is gone...yep gone to waist...my waist. No No...kind sir I lost 4 pounds because I chew very slowly, and process food in my mouth before swallowing. People, if you chewed food slowly, and really let the salvia do its job, you will lose weight.

I am putting in a collect call to TEACHER...what do you mean that line is busy? HaHA very funny!!! There you are...I was a little concerned that it's been over two weeks since we talked last.

WE AS ON HAVE BEEN VACANT LONGER.

Yeah, I know sometimes months...when I was younger...but I am older in years now.

FACTUAL STATEMENT UNRELATED TO COMMUNICATION PROCESSES.

Well, maybe for you but not for me...besides don't get me confused, and I forget what I wanted to talk with you about.

YOUR THOUGHTS ARE CONVOLUTED AND COMPLEX TO GET FACTUAL ANSWERS.

Okay but don't cut me off not yet okay...let me try to get my questions in a logical format. Just listen don't respond okay for a few minutes... I as a human you know we are a very convoluted complex species filled with illogical emotions behavior and sometimes that clouds or masks the logic of perceptions, choices and even beneficial decisions that we should logically make. In other words it is damn hard to be a human sometimes, so we go through moods, or mood swings or periods of days, weeks, months... even years, and yes sometimes never getting out of that "mental slump." TEACH, do you understand anything I am saying

PREDOMINATELY AFFIRMATIVE AS OUR HUMAN BEHAVIOR RECORDS DESCRIBE HOW WE WERE BEFORE MODIFICATION AND THE DATA OF MANY EVALUATED HUMANS CORRELATE TO YOUR STATEMENTS.

You could have just said yes...and that would been fine, but I understand your information, so thanks. So do you understand when I say I do not logically know what I feel right now and what would be the most logical course of action to take.

CONVOLUTIONS OF LOGIC AND ILLOGIC PRODUCE ILLOGICAL CONFLICTS THAT ARE PRESENTLY MOOT TO CALCULATE.

You got that right...I could not said it any better myself. So, asking what do I do is moot, and just actually unintentionally adds to the anxiety.

NOT ALL COMMUNICATIONS ARE MOOT.

True...sometimes it just helps to talk it out with someone.

AFFIRMATIVE.

Be careful TEACH, sounds like you may be getting emotional.

YOUR COMMUNICATION OF ILLOGICAL AND LOGICAL OPTIONS IS LOGICAL.

Okay, okay...you win...you have no emotions.

DATA RECORDS RECORDED THEM.

Do you miss what the data records recorded?

NOT LOGICAL.

TEACHER, if anywhere inside your being I caused a feeling of illogical emptiness, I did not intend to and I apologize for any uncomfortable feelings for you or your kind.

NOT A LOGICAL FEASIBILITY OF EVENTS FOR US AS ONE.

Good...glad to hear you are just as logical as you always were.

YOUR ENDORPHINS ARE ELEVATED.

Good maybe I'll get out of this mental fog soon.

PHYSICAL LOGICALLY FEASIBLE.

I think when we close I'll have a glass of red wine and some of that dark chocolate I have been saving to celebrate that event.

HORMONAL INDUCTIONS PREDOMINATELY ELEVATE YOUR DOPAMINE PRODUCTION.

Want to join me?

NOT FEASIBLE.

Well I'll have a glass of wine for you and your kind's good health as the old saying goes.

NOT LOGICAL TO OUR PHYSICAL STATUS.

Night TEACHER...thanks for listening....

Thus ended the conversation, no linger white noise and time to get that wine and find that dark chocolate bar buried in the refrigerator...hot damn it has cherries in it. Gosh it's hard...oh well I'll just lick it till it warms up.

There seems to be some loose threads on the ends of things I am perceiving as if they are real or not? The reality of one is not always the reality of another, my dear fellow. True, but if a lot of people ae seeing the same thing at the same time isn't that a logical conclusion that that part is real?

Not always true John, as you and we all know that mass hypnosis is very feasible and practical in just about any bizarre encounter. Which brings me to one very important subject I wanted to talk with TEACHER about when people see UFO's...is it mass hypnosis and we see what "THEY" want us to see?

In my many schoolings I have been very well trained and adaptive at hypnosis in counseling people who have been traumatized by many different offenders, abusers and self-inflicted conflicts and irrational counter-behavioral actions. So hypnosis is no stranger to me, and what I did not cover very much in any of my other writings is the power of sound to "induce" hypnosis. I'll probably cover that more in the blog postings that I plan to generate later.

Hi Teach it has only been a few days since we talked last...are you keeping tabs on me just because I am getting older?

NEGATIVE AS THAT IS NOT REQUIRED AS YOUR TRANSMISSIONS ARE STRONGER AND SUMMONED US AS ONE.

Well, there is something I wanted to discuss just for my understanding of things a little better...it is not a wow factor communication like some of the other stuff we have discussed. It's about people in masses seeing what they call UFO or you know flying saucers like your star ships.

SIGHTINGS ARE PREDOMINATELY A MATTER OF PERCEPTIONS.

Yes, and it is that "predominance" that I want to discuss...basically do the people see what is there?

PERCEPTION TOO MANY IS REAL.

I understand that it is real to them...what I am asking you very factually are people seeing what is there or are they seeing a mass hypnosis induced event that is staged for the mass observers?

PREDOMINATELY EVENTS ARE AS PERCEIVED AS MASS HYPNOSIS IS NOT RATIONAL REQUIREMENT.

Okay, sister...why? Why so many sightings and NOT one documented landing where you say "take me to your Leader." There are over 4 million confirmed sightings of UFO from all over the planet.

SIBLINGS IS NOT FACTUAL AS TO NUMBER OF DOCUMENTS ARE NOT ALWAYS US AS ONE.

I think I understand that you are saying these sightings and encounters are not always you and your kind even though you are keeping a very close observation of the humans on earth. I even understand that maybe a very important part of your mission to make sure man-kind survives and all that, but when are you and your kind officially going to make yourself known to the world...not to just the very select few that are in agreements with you now?

COMPLEX QUESTION WITH MANY FACTUAL STATEMENTS REQUIRED FOR UNDERSTANDING AND ACCEPTANCE.

TEACH, do not piss me off by just making short bullet statements, I am wanting a conversation with you.

YOUR ILLOGICAL EMOTIONS OF DESIRES ARE BEING ANSWERED IN FACTUAL STATEMENTS.

Okay, by that statement I will make my desires to communicate very short and blunt to you. Are you the predominate documented sighting producer... that is a simple yes/no answer.

YES.

Are the OTHERS that I have been in communication the next predominate source of documented sightings?

PREDOMINATE YES.

As far as you and your kind know for a fact, not counting you, or the OTHERS are there more than 5 other extraterrestrial beings producing any of these documented sightings? That is a yes/no answer.

PREDOMINATELY YES.

Good now we are getting to know more. Are there more than 10...again a simple yes/no answer.

PREDOMINATELY NO.

Alright there are more than 5 and less than 10 that you know of for a fact that produce these documented sightings.

PREDOMINATELY AFFIRMATIVE.

Are they all that you know of originally from our galaxy?

PREDOMINANTLY YES AS OTHERS ARE NOT.

So most are but, a few are not?

AFFIRMATIVE.

Are any time travelers?

PREDOMINATE YES.

So most more than 50% are time travelers?

PREDOMINATELY YES AS TIME MODIFICATION IS A REQUIREMENT.

So almost all or is it all manipulate time and space.

TIME SPACE MANIPULATION IS A PRIMARY TECHNOLOGICAL REQUIREMENT OF CELESTIAL VISITORS.

Gosh a Mosses, we are so far non-advanced than our visitors.

PREDOMINATELY AFFIRMATIVE AS YOUR SPECIES IS LESS ADVANCED THAN MANY AND MORE THAN MANY IN THE UNIVERSE.

Will we have space time manipulation technology in this century?

DATA INDICATES HUMAN MATTER TRANSFERENCE IN TIME AND SPACE WILL PRIMARILY IN RESEARCH PHASE AT THE BEGINNING OF NEXT CENTURY.

Isn't that also the time of the very probable asteroid impact by your data records?

PREDOMINATELY AFFIRMATIVE AS THE PENDING IMPACT DELAYS THE TIME SPACE DEVELOPMENT.

Understood...Teach thanks for the information how about we close for now however, do it pig Latin style understood? And simple yes/no....

YES.

Gotcha...there was slight mental white noise static when TEACHER broke the connection and I am almost positive our conversation about visitors were monitored. Hey dudes, I know you are there listening in and that is not nice to be an ease dropper without officially saying hello---mind if we listen in? The answer is I do not mind just have the respect to say you want to listen. Hell, I'd be glad if you threw in your 5 cents worth (used to be 2 cents but, inflation).

Yes...I am very aware of the "programming" that is doing the "allegorical" into the so-called Artificial Intelligence." That buddy is NOT a zinger to me...it IS to the 99.9999999% of the world populace. AI to have any real humanity value needs to be as I wrote about...remove the GREED or the bias of these damn programs as how evaluations of data is validated. IF we don't we WILL be SORRY!

Please remember intelligence is intelligence (zeros/ones), but, without WISDOM IT (Intelligence Technology), is chaotic devastating to the world populace and the planet.

This I plan on more writing about in my blog...I pray the warnings are logically evaluated for the importance to man-kind. Please GC do not allow man-kind's perceived need for greed to over-run and over prioritize the human kind's and the planet's true needs. This I implore you to Universally intercede and make man-kind do the right thing for once. I think from what I can derive from TEACHER that is why there is a long delay before her and her kind actually co-habit earth and eventually beyond.

Later:

What the HELL! Why am I in a hospital, with an IV in my arm, with a plus/ox gismo on my finger and...holy cow I got EKG leads going to two sets of monitors, and a beep pause beep machine showing my heart rate???

Talk about abduction all I remember I was talking to a nurse as she was putting on my BP cuff for my yearly check up...that was...damn.... when was that? Well, the big clock on the wall says it is almost time for some famous hospital food. I know how sick they think I am by the food they bring me. Hell with that I calling the nurse...where's that buzzer....oh yeah its tied into the TV corded remote.

A few seconds later my room is full of people including some old Indian dude saying that they think I had a stroke while talking to the nurse in the doctor's office but I didn't seem to have normal stroke symptoms. I asked what are normal stroke symptoms? He rattled of a bunch of stuff, that they use FACE as a checklist to get a general idea. However my MRI/CAT scan and EKG, and EEG all looked acceptable for a person my age (actually a little younger), and they could not find any causes.

Well, now that I am awake and in their world I have a very good idea what happened. I'll tell it in a "flashback" like they do in movies....NO smart-ass I did not say Hot Flash as in male menopause!

The doctor said I was talking to the nurse as she was checking my blood pressure and I just went "blank"...scared the crap out of the young nurse in the doctor's office. She said, "He looked gone, but he was there physically...he just was not responding to anything." She yelled fort the doctor, they called 911 and here I am in a Catholic named chain hospital. I asked about insurance and they said they made copies of my insurance cards from the doctors office. They said I had good insurance policies.

I was discharged a few hours later...never got to see what hospital meal I was going to have and told to see the doctor in two weeks for a follow-up MRI or call 911 if any relapse.

Okay time for the flashback......rewind the film pleas to the scene in the doctors office and the nurse was putting on the BP cuff......

"I feel actually pretty good most days...my goal is to stay just a notch above".......blank city for me and the nurse....well, not blank city for me. I am in that abandoned warehouse again and the light with the OTHER is forming.

I could not tell them I was visiting the OTHERS and getting information discussed about the treatment of humans while being "evaluated" now could I. You and I both know where my next room would be in that hospital...how do you like your rubber, and that nice leather formed fitting jacket with all the buckles....Oh were are sorry the Torazine shot in the butt hurts. Next time we will consider Haldol...No Thank You...that is not my idea of a mind blowing cocktail. Besides it makes the orange juice taste like castor oil and sardines, with just a hint of garlic....I bet no vampire dames will date me for a while.

That said I did have a very informative communication with the OTHER that was assigned to me. I think we may have actually designed an agreement that would be better for future human evaluations/abductions. I think I will continue most of that in the blog to be started soon....hopefully.

The OTHERS are a very unique breed as I have already told you some information about them. This last visit where I was with the OTHERS mentally and physically I was in the neurological ICU ward at the hospital was a very "interesting trip for my mind and body." The me, myself and I and all the others in my gut were all being manipulated, tested, probed and having a very intense telepathic conversation all at the same time. I am almost positive I do NOT want any parts of my being to experience that ever again. Even though thank the Great Creator I was not harmed in any way which was damn lucky for me as Haldol and god knows what other blood-letting lobotomy technology was going to be used on me while I was conversing with the OTHERS. All for the benefit of those future abductees not to experience such traumatic events and remember them where they cause virtually life-long mental and physical conflicts. Some physical manifestations are direct results of the perceived fear during an abduction or evaluation as they call it.

As I said the OTHERS' eyes are very unique as the physical link that moves them together side/side, up/down and also correlates to the back eye as well in the brain. Their brain looks a lot like a cross between a human and reptiles actually a well developed fish. See the illustrations.

Why can not TEACHER and her kind be involved in these very critical communications with us?

THEY ARE NOT A REQUIREMENT OF OUR EVALUATIONS.

Well, they sure are a priority of mine, especially since I have been with her practically all my human life this time around.

NO EVALUATION CRITERIA FOR UNNEEDED ENTITIES IN THE HUMAN EVALUATIONS.

I know you as your species do not have the need for evaluating TEACHER and her kind, but logically she and her kind were humans before the modification of their DNA, regardless that she and her kind abduct or evaluate humans just like you do only your evaluation criteria's are different but realistically they are very similar as to determining the strength of the human DNA chain.

CONVOLUTED LOGIC AND ILLOGIC AS PREPONDERANCE OF EVALUATION FACTUAL DATA.

Sorry, but I am totally lost on that answer?

UNNEEDED ENTITIES HISTORY IS NOT A CRITERIA REQUIREMENT.

That I understand for you, and I would logically surmise the true is for TEACHER and her kind in correlating data to your evaluation criteria's. However, the fact still remains that you both two separate species evaluate humans for the DNA strain strength because you both influenced and modified the natural human evolutional process...did you not.

HUMAN DNA EVOLUTION MODIFICATION WAS ESSENTIAL FOR TIME EVENT SEGMENTS.

I know that and actually I am glad you and TEACHER did influence and modify our natural evolutional process...because I feel logically we would not be having this conversation we are having in this time segment.

PREDOMINATELY AFFIRMATIVE AS THE HUMAN WOULD BE IN A DIFFERENT TIME REALM OF ADVANCEMENT.

Alright one last time I will ask this...is it more logical to include TEACHER and her kind in these conversations or not especially since both your different species influenced and modified the human species normal evolution process....how do you know that logically your modification or TEACHER modification at a different time did NOT significantly affect your evaluation results. I do not logically think you can prove or disprove that.

And now I am in the hospital bed and you know what happened then. Gosh when the OTHERS shut off there is no easing out like with TEACHER...it is BAM we are out of here...right where you were. IF I am on the toilet, I am going to be pissed...very pissed...literally!!!

What do you mean it is not required? I busted my ass trying to get you in on the conversations with the OTHERS and you tell me you don't need to be there.

AFFIRMATIVE AS OUR DNA EVALUATIONS ARE NOT THE SAME MISSION REQUIREMENT OF THE OTHERS YOU COMMUNICATE WITH.

TEACHER you can get pissed at me or not....don't talk yet....I know you do not have the anger emotion, but by GOD I do! And I am going to express it in no pull punches way... It is going to be full of emotion and if you tell me I am emotional I am going to figure out some way to reach out and punch you in the face...got that! Do NOT say a word yet! I will take a deep breath here and present this logically with a lot of piss and vinegar behind the logic.

Logically you both as separate species at one time or another influenced modified or what is called interfered with the normal human evolutional process because of certain events that would happen at certain times. Logically you both determine the strength of human DNA which don't forget you and your kind once were. It does NOT matter at all logically what specific little evaluation testing system you as two separate species choose to evaluate the DNA strain. You both want to know what are the strength factors for some survival criteria. Am I correct so far...you can speak now.

PREDOMINATELY YOUR CONVOLUTED LOGICAL AND ILLOGICAL ASSUMPTIONS ARE AFFIRMATIVE.

You better be glad you said that because I was going to really get pissed at the whole lot of you, your kind, the OTHERS and whomever is listening in and tell you ALL to go fuck yourselves!...Don't say it!

Okay...logically is it more productive to you and your kind to wait and see what are the results of my conversations with the OTHERS than have you involved?

PREDOMINATELY AFFIRMATIVE AS TO LOGICAL CROSS FEEDS ARE ILLOGICAL.

I agree...I would be very confused listening to you two talk logic and try to understand what is being said. It is hard...very difficult for me to understand your logic communications. I can just imagine what it would be like trying to understand two of your non-emotional logic communicators.

YES, AS LOGICAL ASSUMPTION OF AN ILLOGICAL EMOTION REACTANT BEING.

Damn, once again, my illogical emotional brain got overly emotional and I felt all that I tried to do was being given no value...especially by you...since I do place a lot of belief and faith in what you say and teach me...as I know I will always be the hot-headed soft rock student.

YOUR HUMAN DEVELOPMENT IS PROGRESSING AT AN ACCEPTABLE MANNER.

Well at least you are not taking me out behind the chicken house and using the screen wire fly swatter with its broken pieces of wire sticking out on my back and legs.

THAT IS NOT LOGICAL.

That's what I tried to get them to understand...

How about we just slowly close out as I am somewhat drained from being so upset with....well, to be honest upset at myself...mostly, and whomever is listen in if you are say whatever in the hell you want...I'll evaluate it for it is worth to me logically.

Chicken-shit coward...don't even have the respect... or if you have balls to come forward...out in the open.....not even a zinger!

Well, maybe there was a zinger and I did not catch it totally as we closed out as it I think said parallel universes." That makes me think of all those different sifi movies I saw on time travel and other dimensional worlds. There were several TV shows about time travel and parallel worlds. So I wonder what TEACHER or even maybe the OTHERS have to say about us humans and parallel worlds? Does influencing this human terrafirma DNA evolutional location influence or modify any other locations...and if so why and if so why-NOT? Those seem like some very heavy questions and may need to be covered more in the blog as well if not covered or at least introduced here.

TEACHER remember when we spoke about the various universes were like on a figure"8" never ending and never beginning and no matter how small you sliced it... it was always going to be there?

PARALLELS OF EXISTENCES EXIST IN ALL REALMS AND DIMENSIONS.

Yes, why or how is this Erath's human DNA modification you and OTHERS have admitted to doing to make certain events happen at certain times in keeping with that natural course of events or recorded documents of history accurate or traceable?

CONVOLUTED ASSUMPTIONS OF FACTUAL EVENTS ARE NOT ILLOGICAL EVENTS.

Wait...wait just a minute here...I refuse to get angry at what you are saying because I know I can misunderstand things that you say very easily, and that made absolutely no sense to me at all...please explain in more detail.

SPACE TIME REALM OF TARGET LOCATION IS MANDATORY COORDINATOR AS NO OTHER LOCATION CAN BE THE MANDATORY COORDINATOR LOCATION.

I think you are saying that this earth within all the different parallels is the only one that was DNA modified by you and the OTHERS at specific times but were always on this earth's location.

PREDOMINATELY AFFIRMATIVE AS WE AS ONE ONLY THIS LOCATION AS OTHERS MODIFIED VARIOUS SPECIES DNA.

Are you saying the OTHERS also modified different animals on earth in addition to humans?

AFFIRMATIVE.

Okay...um...how about on......

PREDOMINATELY AFFIRMATIVE AS TO OTHER LOCATIONS SPECIES DNA MODIFICATIONS.

WOW! The OTHERS modified other worlds DNA.....please tell me there were no humans and was only fish, snails and bugs and stuff.

NEGATIVE.

TEACHER that is not fair what do you mean negative...were there other human species in other parallel earths or worlds that were DNA modified or not?

NEGATIVE AS TO NO FACTUAL DOCUMENTATION OF DNA MODIFICATIONS BY OTHERS THAT YOU COMMUNICATE WITH OR OTHERS THAT YOU DO NOT COMMUNICATE WITH.

Are you saying more advanced races like you and your kind, the OTHERS that I have communicated with and with the they, them, GREYS or others have modified various species on different worlds and in different time lines virtually whenever they chose too?

PREDOMINATELY AFFIRMATIVE.

My gosh, I am too stunned to be emotionally pissed, upset, or even not surprised at having what I have suspected for years be confirmed by you.

PREDOMINANCE OF FACTUAL EVENTS IS DESIGNED TO PRODUCE FACTUAL CONCLUSIONS.

Unhun... whatever...... you say...is the entire universe a giant Guinea Pig laboratory for the more advanced species to play upon the lesser advanced species?

ILLOGICAL STATEMENT.

Well maybe it is illogical but I got my factual logical answer from what you just said.

FACTUAL STATEMENTS ARE TO BE UNDERSTOOD.

Look TEACHER I am not mad or anything...

NOT A LOGICAL STATEMENT.

Okay...how about we just close for now...I need a cold beer and some low carbo pizza to help me chew on all this information.

Holy cow reader...do you realize what we just learned? I'll just use one question mark here because some of the next stuff will require more than one question mark and hopefully, I'll be able to get detailed up-to-date information to you the readers of my blog. However, that said, I will be really depending upon you the readers to provide comments/feed-back or as they say "likes/or dislikes" to help keep me on track. That being said, you know as well as I do that most of the comments will not affect me one way or another, because I am just the messenger...and it is entirely up to you do deal with or not deal with the information I provide you. You know I will pull no punches and I will do my best to tell it as TEACHER, the OTHERS and the THEM, THEY, and the GREYS tell me... I am not going to present the news from one political slant or another...other than what "slant you already should know I am prone to" and that is no unneeded bull dust or fluff.

TEACHER, I need you to get down and as truthful as you can about this Mono-Polarity stuff especially since many humans do not know or realize that magnetic forces are the most predominated strongest forces in our universes. Just like many people do not realize the sun's our sun/star magnetic bands are what produces solar winds and when magnetic bands cross which we are told does not happen but IT DO and when it does the electromagnetic fireworks produce the massive Cornea ejections...that TEACH is billions of tons of energy/matter than any atomic bomb we have. The only thing protecting earth is a magnetic force field that is not even as strong as the refrigerator magnet.

POSITION IS NOT REQUIRED TO TRANSMIT FACTUAL STATEMENTS.

Yep I know...figure of speech, now I need you to tell me everything you know about what I call Mono-Polarity and if you call it something what do you call it and why?

MONO AS IN ONE IS PREDOMINATELY A FACTUAL HYPOTHESIS OF THE MAGNETIC EVENT YOU ARE SEEKING.

So there is a single magnetic polarity action within a magnetic field and it is NOT just limited to a dual pole action?

PREDOMINATELY NEGATIVE AS THE DUAL POLE IS THE MAJORITY OF THE ACTION OF THE SINGLE DUALITY ACTION.

Okay let's see if the soft rock understood what you just said...that most or a greater part of the magnetic field is a dual pole action and that the North and South Pole is determined by the flow direction of the electrons within the magnetic field. Is that correct so far?

PREDOMINATELY AFFIRMATIVE.

Okay so there is some tweaking here and there but that is the basic...is this down to molecular level?

NEGATIVE AS THE MOLECULAR LEVEL IS NOT THE FINITE DIVIDER OF THE DUALITY POLARITY.

So it is something even smaller than the molecular level as in sub molecular or atomic level?

IN YOUR PERCEPTION SUBATOMIC IS NOT CORRECT.

Whoa...are you saying I am perceiving what sub-atomic means incorrectly?

PRIMARILY AFFIRMATIVE AS YOUR PERCEPTION OF SUBATOMIC IS NOT COMPLETE TO THE LEVEL OF THE MONO DUALITY DIVISION EVENT.

Okay TEACH this is getting really deep into the atom and my understanding what the atom is with its nuclei and electron orbits surrounding the atom. I am somewhat very aware of what we call quarks quasars, bosons, mesons and other little pieces of the sub-atomic nuclei compositions...and maybe some little bits and pieces that I know of but don't understand them as of yet from all the so-called experts.

SCANNING YOUR MEMORY DATA IS PREDOMINATELY CORRECT AS THERE ARE DATA PORTIONS MISSING FROM THE MONO-DUALITY DIVISION EVENT.

You keep referring to a mono-duality division event...to me that is a contradictory of terms however, if I perceive it from your words it is where two somethings split into one single even going its own way. Is that correct?

PREDOMINATELY AFFIRMATIVE AS THE EVENTS TRAVERSE IN ALL TANGENTS AT ONCE TO PROVIDE THE DUALITY BONDING ACTION.

Holy cow TEACH I understand what you just said...that is HUGE to understanding Mono-Polarity behavior...THANKS...THANK YOU SO VERY MUCH!

YOUR ENDORPHINS ARE ELEVATING AS IN PLEASURE HORMONES.

You bet your sweet bippy they are!

WHAT IS BIPPY?

1960's Hippie slang for your ass/butt! It is a positive worthwhile expression.

WE AS ONE WILL ADD THAT EXPRESSION TO OUR DATA BANKS AS TO A SWEET SMELLING RECTUM HUMAN EXPRESSION OF JOY.

That's funny TEACH...Yeah, that's close enough...sweet smelling ass.

TEACHER, I have to close on that comment of yours...it is so damn funny and I need to really think and understand what you just shared with me...and our readers...as we are the only ones who know about this, for now??

Let's get back to that big little hint that I gave you about magnetic force fields and what makes everything tick. I am not talking about Mono-Polarity here...I am talking about the energy and power that "shines" on us thank the GC every nano-second of our existence. However, remember where I said an earth magnetic force field that is "Less" stronger than your average refrigerator magnet or that "rolled magnetic" strip even on some business cards and other forms of advertisements. But those car magnetic signs are a lot stronger as far as griping holding power to the metal surface.

Just think a very weak magnetic force field is what is preventing the earth from being another MARS atmosphere. Think of that statement for what IT really means to the entire earth's survival...now the 64 trillion dollar question...why can't we greedy capitalist humans use that technology that we presently have to start to harness the power/energy that is there free for the taking or manipulating.

Just one massive mirror system to collect one of those massive solar flare or even a CME (Corona Mass Ejection). For GOD sakes do not put a plutonium bomb in Jupiter to make it another sun like some of the scientific thinking fools want to do. Do you know why? They want Neptune and Uranus and other planets in our solar system to have a "sun." UR ANUS is what these jerks are thinking with.

I am not going to cover a lot more on the very important magnetic force fields of masses. I hope to cover this in-depth in my blogs.

Are these blogs I mentioned of interest to you???

WHAT IF I have not written about a lot of subjects that I have had with TEACHER and her kind, the OTHERS, and as I said the THEM, THEY, and GREYS. WHAT IF I only write about ½ of what has been shared.

WHAT IF?????????????????

.>Q.Z

ET-BEINGS 10/8 OTHERS HEART AND LUNGS 2018:   this is a close representative of the larger lungs and heart with the dual arties and veins that feed into larger lungs. The bronical tube is slightly visible in this drawing.

The heart in relationship to human is about 2/3 larger and the lungs are about 200%. The blood flow is at about 210/130 BP and 28 pints of blood move through the OTHERS body very rapidly.

The 02 and methane exchange rate is much faster than a human and the C02 exchange is also mixed with Chromium and more nitrogen with some Sulphur.

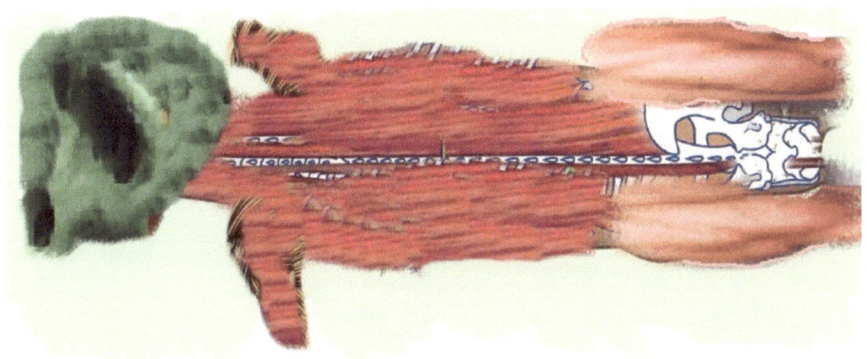

.>Q.Z

ET-BEINGS 10/8 OTHERS BACK AND BODY LAYOUT 1A 2018:

The skull is twisted to show the single long eye orbital socket in relationship to the back and neck muscles. Notice the legs are at the side and not in the full extended position.

This top back view shows the approx. layout of the OTHERS legs when not extended as in the lower biped walking position. The elevated biped walking position places the OTHERS creature at approx. 7 feet tall.

The lower part of the split legs folds up and under the area of the knee to provide the "hunched" walking appearance. As the knee and hip joint rotates the OTHERS to its full upright walking running position...this is when the species is 7 feet+ tall.

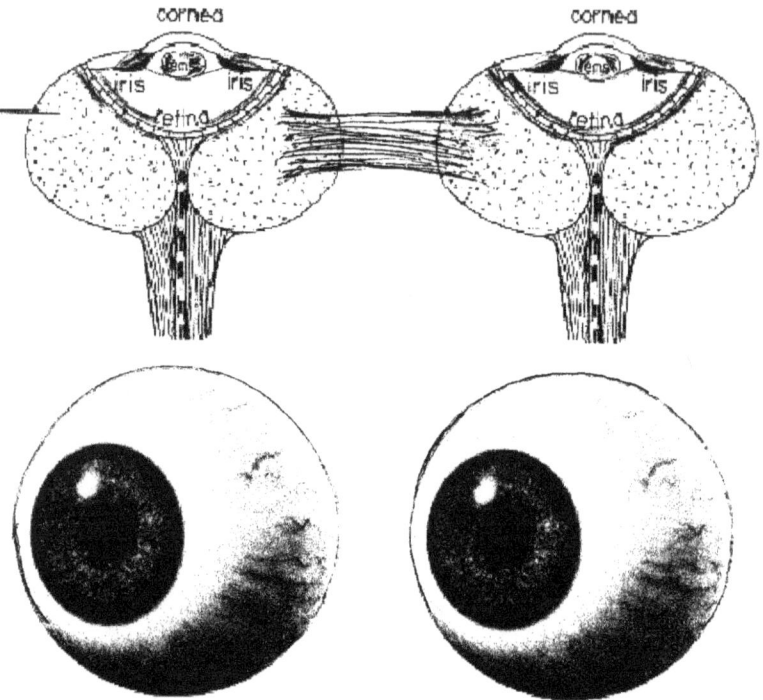

ET-BEINGS OTHERS EYES / HUMAN EYES 1A 2018:

This shows the human eyes compared to the OTHERS dual eyes that linked by a thick optic nerve fiber bundle. The eye is also somewhat elongated and the inner and outer iris shows as it reflects all images especially the extended peripheral vision upon the OTHERS retina area. The OTHERS retina macula fine focus are is a lot wider than the human eye area.

The OTHERS dual eye also has a very thin vitreous fluid that is not as thick as the human eye and this allows the entire eyeball to adjust in size as to just about any special viewing requirements.

The rods/cones of the eye are much more into the infrared and ultraviolet areas and this is only in the front as the rear eye is not this sensitive to these hues...much like aa human eye spectrum range.

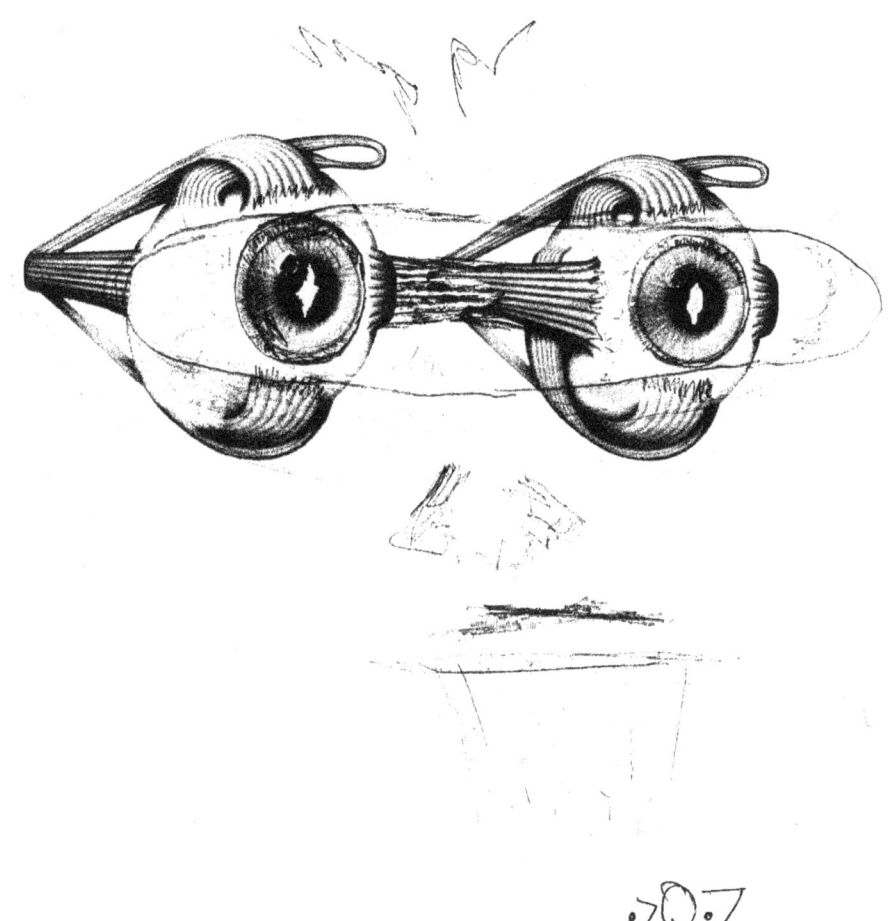

ET-BEINGS 10/8 OTHERS DUAL EYES IN SOCKET 2018: This shows the inner muscle nerve bundle that connects the two eyes together and the reflective out iris that increases the peripheral field of vision by almost 300 degrees as a very pure clean "fish-eye lens and clear frontal and side vision at the same time. The rear single eye is constructed the same way with one single optic nerve bundle to the rear of the enlarged brain and brain stem.

The dual eyes are attached to a very strong nerve fiber network that moves both eyes at the same time. This dual movement in a single eye orbit socket is totally separate from the rear eye movement and if you view the brain illustration you will see the three separate optic nerves are attached to the enlarged elongated brain and brain stem that attaches to the spinal column.

Each eye is focused and works independently and also in unison with the other eye to provide a very unique optical visual plain of not just 3 D but also a much wider peripheral view that gives a cleaner and more functional "fisheye lens" viewing effect. This extended peripheral fish-eye viewing offers a cleaner and sharper 3D that is almost 3D in all axis at once.

TEACHER's reflective lens does some of this wider viewing as well. Remember how she and her kind have two eyes inside one and the large reflective protective lens projects the images into on focal point.

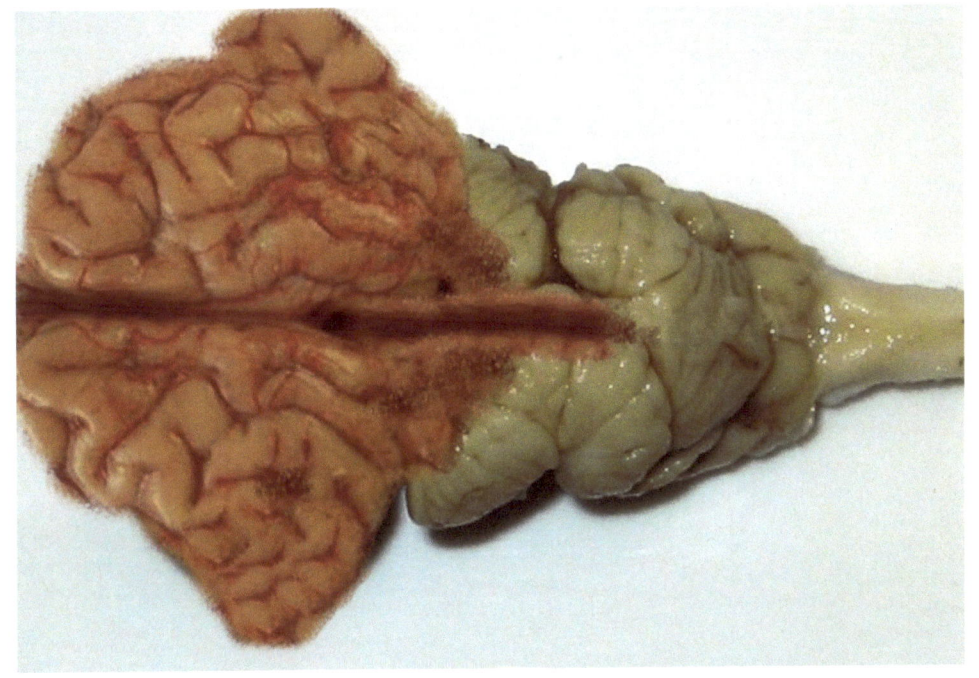

.>Q.Z

OTHER'S BRAIN with Optic Nerves 1A 2018: This is the OTHERS brain with its increased wider lobes and the brain stem that is more tannish in color. The third eye is attached to the elongated brownish optic nerve. The eyes are not shown in this illustration. The brain stem actually tilts downward and connects to the spinal cord.

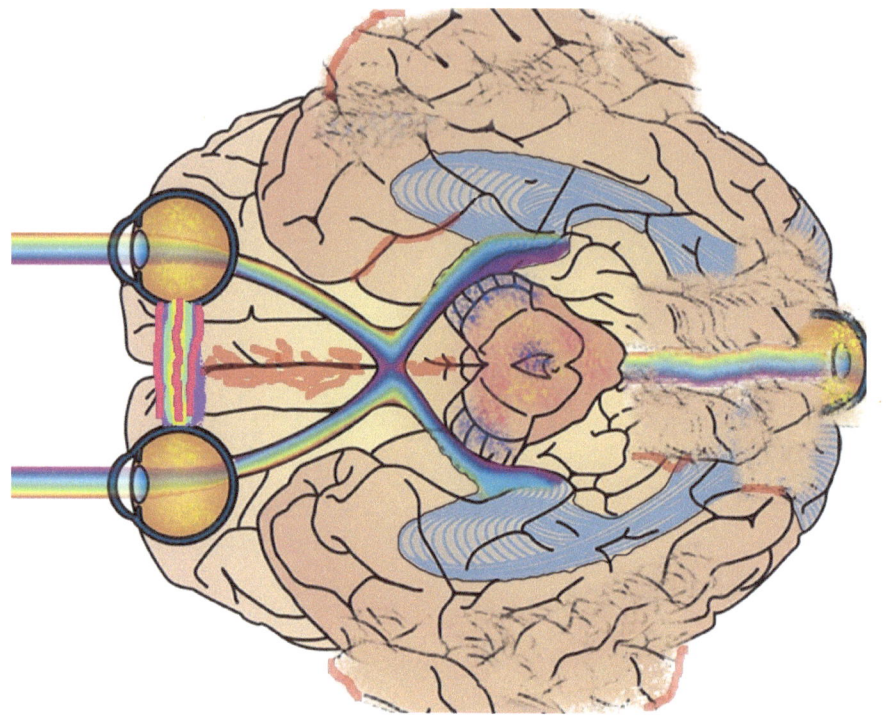

.>Q.Z

ET-BEINGS 10/8 OTHERS BRAIN AND OPTIC NERVES SYSTEM:
This is the OTHERS brain with eyes and optic nerve placement in the brain. You will note the brain stem is not shown but the Corpus Callosum is somewhat shown and it is wider, thicker with many prominent connector points.

OTHERS SPECIES DRAWINGS: I do not want these super clear because I am not sure the images I perceived were totally accurate so, I am leaving some "wiggle" buffer room for possible errors but, I think these are close.

Leg
extended
fully

MUltiple
ARMS / Legs
positions

7QZ

Chin chewer
VAPOR filter

Can walk/run
on 2 or 4 limbs/legs

Totally
Reversed

Able to "Rise" from
3½'-6't and then
20 t to ...

⚬X⚬Q⚬Z

young
OTHERS

10-14 days
old

on all 8
ARMS
Legs

ON
All 4s
3/4
extended

WALKS On UPRIGHT on 4 Legs
or all 8

REAR
eye
BACK Head

⊃Q·Z

⊃Q·Z

EPILOG...

WHAT IF
&
BEYOND!!!!

Dear Reader if you read any of the ET-BEINGS books/series please review on Amazon.com. Also you may want to visit my web site at **et-beings.com** for more information, and the latest on my blogs etc.

Thank You...Blessed Be

·>☐·☐

John Q. Zarr